FERMENTATION

FERMENTATION

ANGELICA J.

Grove Press
New York

Published simultaneously in Canada
Printed in the United States of America
Originally published in Great Britain by Bloomsbury Publishing Plc

FIRST AMERICAN EDITION

J., Angelica.
Fermentation / Angelica J. — 1st Grove Press ed.
p.   cm.
ISBN 0-8021-1614-0
I. Title.
PS3560.A2476F47   1997
813'.54—dc21   97-10198

Grove Press
841 Broadway
New York, NY 10003

1 3 5 7 9 10 8 6 4 2

Behold, I saw upon earth men carrying milk in earthen vessels and making cheeses therefrom. Some was of the thick kind from which firm cheese is made, some of the thinner sort from which more porous cheese is made, and some was mixed with corruption and of the sort from which bitter cheese is made. And I saw the likeness of a woman having a complete human form within her womb . . . Men and women alike, having in their bodies the seed of mankind from which are procreated the various kinds of human beings. Part is thickened because the seed in its strength is well and truly concocted and this produces forceful men to whom are allotted gifts both spiritual and carnal . . . And some had cheese less firmly curdled, for in their feebleness they have seed imperfectly tempered and they raise offspring mostly stupid, feeble and useless.

from the Liber Scivias *of St Hildegard*
(translated by Singer)

In the womb of a mother was I moulded . . . being compacted with blood of the seed of man and the pleasure that accompanieth sleep.

Wisdom of Solomon (vii, 2)

FERMENTATION

PRELUDE

Two things marked that long summer out. The first was the heat. It had crept up on us in the early days of April, starting with the dry silent winds from East Africa that blew in across the sea, then moved stealthily upwards over the country until they reached the city and came to rest like a tight shroud. The moon and stars burned, the grass in the city's gardens gradually turned brown and the flowers were all but devoured. A plague of red caterpillars hatched out in their thousands. Some people said their eggs had been blown in with the winds and that they would spread disease. The city's pestilence-control teams tried to contain the outbreak by spraying but the creatures did not die. Instead all the flowers shrivelled and the trees grew thin and faded. The river's water level dropped. Earth turned to dust, woodwork splintered and the sky remained a hot, pearly blue.

There was no break to the heat, no let-up, no relief, and finally no renewal.

The second thing that marked that summer out was the strike. The refuse men were in dispute with local

3

government. The papers said the strikers could not hold out for longer than two weeks, but after two months there were no signs that the end was in sight. The rubbish piled up; outside the restaurants rotting food spilled over into the gutters: fish heads, mouldy vegetables, lumps of fat, babies' nappies, green meat and rancid milk all littered the streets and grew putrid in the heat.

Most of the city's inhabitants had closed their doors and shutters and left for the hills and the mountains where the snow never melted or the coast where the breeze was still fresh. Those who remained had seen rats; thousands of them scrabbling along the pavements, nesting in the rubbish.

At night I would lie in bed with no covers and the windows wide open, praying for a breeze to pass over my skin. But the air did not stir. It was heavy with the sweet scent of rotting food and there were times I believed it would suffocate me in my sleep. It twisted around my throat like a rope and left me hanging in the night for breath. That is when I began to write it all down. During these long broken nights I would wake in a pool of sweat and write down the dreams in the notebook I kept on my bedside table. The book was full of ideas for stories, and lists of words I liked, things I had seen, strange sentences I heard people say in passing on the street. Now I began to write down my dreams. They were very vivid, like short films with a story to tell. I could remember them in detail on waking, and at first it was this intensity that caused me to record them in my notebook. Later it wasn't their clarity that kept me writing; the writing down was the reason for my having them in the first place. There was a definite cause, a pattern if you like, which it took me a while to work out but once detected was indeed very simple.

Let us say then, to begin with, that different women crave different things. I read once of a woman who ate coal. At night, when her husband and children were asleep, she would creep down into the cellar in order to suck on the cold, dark lumps of rock. Then there was the woman who smelt neat disinfectant: she bought huge plastic containers of bleach so she could sniff the invisible liquid on pads of cottonwool which she kept secreted in her pockets. Anne Boleyn ate larks' tongues. Fabienne, the girl in the apartments opposite, kept a large tank of catfish. She would cut off their heads and eat the bodies raw. My mother told me of an African woman who ate termite mounds, preferably after it had rained so the earth was moist. Mary Queen of Scots was said to have requested swans' genitals, and one of my aunts on my father's side insisted on smothering pickled onions in golden syrup. It is also recorded that a certain Tibetan princess favoured rats. Then there was Eve and her overwhelming desire for that now infamous piece of fruit.

Whatever; the list is endless and the stories unique. I

had hoped that my craving, should I ever fall pregnant, would be oysters. I had a vision of myself going into the most exclusive restaurants in the city and snapping my fingers at the waiters to bring me the menu. I would be seated in front of a long table with a starched white cloth spread over it and I would order them to serve me with platters of oysters arranged on huge piles of ice. One by one I would split the shells open with my knife and tip their contents into my mouth. I would feel the soft flesh on my tongue and taste their velvety fishiness before swallowing them whole. This I would do day and night whenever the craving took me. If the restaurants weren't open I would simply ask Serge to get up and find me the shellfish, even if it meant crossing the city or travelling the four hundred kilometres or so down to the harbour to wait for the boats to return.

But it wasn't to be. My body chose my craving for me, and oysters weren't on the menu.

BRIE

Brie should feel slightly plump and supple. It should have a mild flavour and ideally its body should be of a rich, pliable consistency. Eat at room temperature and avoid cheeses that are inflexible, have a chemical smell or any that are rheumy.

'Don't eat that,' Serge said, trying to grab the plate out of my hands. 'Not just before going to bed. It will give you bad dreams.' I had returned from the kitchen with a shiny red apple and a huge piece of Brie which lay in its bloomy envelope like thick creamy vellum.

'It's all I feel like eating,' I said. 'Maybe this is my craving.'

'That's an old wives' tale and you know it. It's all in the mind, and besides you've been pregnant for weeks without any strange cravings.'

'My book says that cravings can start at any time during a pregnancy. I want to eat it.'

'Okay,' he said, smiling. 'Cheese. That's not so bad. Do you think it's particularly Brie? I could stock up on it. Buy some of those huge round pieces.'

'I don't know. Brie's all we have in the fridge.'

I went and found a knife and then sat down at the table with my plate. The cheese spread out slightly as I pierced a small segment on my knife. It hadn't reached the stage where it oozed out on to the plate. That was the

9

stage I liked best but Serge always insisted on keeping the cheese refrigerated so it didn't smell out the kitchen. I slipped the piece into my mouth and immediately felt how soft it was and how delicate the taste. While I ate Serge told me a story he had heard from one of his friends a long time ago.

'He said that on a trip to America, Salvador Dali was asked what he thought of New York. "New York," he said, "is like a Gothic Roquefort." He was right, wasn't he?' Serge said. 'It does taste somehow dark and strong. The brownstones, the gargoyles. Anyway, apparently later on during this trip someone else asked what he thought about San Francisco. "San Francisco," he said, "is a romantic Camembert." Just imagine,' Serge said, looking at me while I ate, 'we could build a new language. How would you describe this city?'

I shrugged my shoulders. 'A pastoral Brie?'

'A Dionysian Gloucester?'

'Infernal Gorgonzola.'

'Dublin is like a virginal mozzarella.'

'Copenhagan is a melancholic Comte.'

'Prague is a hedonistic feta.'

'Sybaritic Port Salut.'

'An Emmentalian hole.'

'I love you with a Stiltonic passion,' I said and looked into his eyes.

Later we slipped between the white linen sheets I had been keeping in the icebox and which smelt vaguely of the mushroomy Brie. We lay silently side by side in the dark listening to a thin cat hissing in the street below. I could smell our bodies trying to breathe against the heat. Tiny beads of perspiration silently formed on our skin, dampening the sheets. It was too hot to make love; even to lie like that, skin to skin, made me feel agitated. I edged away from Serge and closed my eyes. At some point I drifted into sleep.

I knelt down by the huge brown animal and with my hot cheek pressed into its rounded flanks let my fingers tease out long lines of milk which hit the metal pail beneath with the satisfying ring of bullets. It was hot and dark inside the milking sheds and the strong sweet smell of the heavy beasts, their milky breath and the hay was making me drowsy. I leant my full weight against the firm body of the animal and closed my eyes. Its skin was soft and warm. Outside I could hear the sound of girls laughing and playing and I wanted to join them in the gardens and the sunlight that I knew lay beyond. The fields were like a paradise: all the buds were splitting, the grass was green and the still air spilled with floating seeds and luminous insects. I knew it all lay beyond the door and yet I stayed in the dark of the sheds. With my strong brown fingers, I pulled methodically at the animal's shuddering sack of milk and watched as the bucket slowly began to fill with the warm frothy liquid. Every now and then I'd dip my finger in and suck on the sweet milk like a child.

When the pail was full I stood up and wiped the

perspiration from my face. My entire body was hot and I could feel tiny rivulets of sweat trickling down the insides of my thighs. The animals around me moved in anticipation and I could see milk oozing from their swollen teats dripping down on to the floor. I lifted the pail and began to walk unevenly across the barn, but as I moved my foot caught on a stone and the bucket jerked from my hands and landed with a clatter. The milk immediately spilled out, forming a large white lake on the dirty stone floor.

'You're very clumsy,' a voice said from inside the barn.

I looked around me and saw a shadow in the far corner.

'Don't you think you ought to clear it up? Get down on your hands and knees and lick.' I hesitated and the voice repeated itself. 'I said get down and lick it up.'

Slowly I put the pail down and crouched on the floor. The stones were cool and smelt mildly of ammonia.

'Lick,' the voice again commanded and I stuck out my tongue and began to lick at the pool, all the time aware of the fact that a man stood in the shadows watching me. Then I heard him cross the barn and felt him prod me from behind with his boot.

'You're far too slow,' he said. 'It will never get cleared up at this rate. Take off your skirts and underclothes and clear it up.'

I stood up slowly and began to slip off my clothing until my lower half was naked. When that was done I felt his hands on my shoulders pushing me down so that I had to squat in the white pool. I began wiping at the milk with my skirts.

'Not with your clothing,' the man said, grabbing my skirts from my hands.

I crouched down lower and immediately could feel the cool milk brushing against my sex. I dragged myself over the floor.

'That's better. Much better,' he said. 'Now get down on all fours like that animal.' I could hear the man crouch down behind me. 'Let me see you drinking from it,' he said, pushing me towards the beast in its stall.

I put my tongue to the warm sack of milk and began to suckle the animal, making my lips work as fingers, tightening and relaxing them to ease out the milk, and all the while I could feel the man's hand touching me between my milky wet legs, stroking and caressing me. The milk dripped from my sex and spilled from my mouth.

'You've made a terrible mess of yourself,' he whispered gently as he moved closer and began to lick the milk from my skin.

I could feel his strong tongue like a giant cat's rasping and flicking up inside me. My body shuddered with short even spasms and I felt myself unfolding like a fat pink bud. I wanted him now, and it was as if he read my desire for at that moment he mounted me and pushed with the full weight of his body deep inside.

In the dark I could hear the animals growing restless,

stamping the ground, waiting. The beast I was drinking from shifted uneasily. My mouth filled again with its warm sweet milk, and as I drank my body heaved with the thrust of the man and the animals' moaning and slowly filled to the brim with thick rich milkiness.

When I awoke I put my hand between my thighs and felt how wet I was. I slipped my fingers inside, then gently drew them out and began to draw tiny circles against my soft wet skin. I hadn't done this for many years but it did not take me long to make myself come.

As a child I had learnt this art by sitting on the fence at the bottom of our garden. I would sit astride it to watch the horses in the field. I liked the way they moved and sometimes my mother gave me sugar-lumps to feed them with and they would come over and press their large velvety noses into the palm of my hand. One day when I was waiting for my friend Alicia to arrive I discovered that if I wriggled around on the fence just a little I could produce a delicious sensation between my legs. At its climax was a relief of such glorious pleasure that I knew I would have to repeat it over and over and I began to experiment. I discovered that, if I did it at around the same time as my mother was cooking in the kitchen, the thought that she might at any moment look out of the window and discover me in the act was the best way to produce the sensation I craved. And then as I grew older my stimuli changed. I realised I did not need the magic fence but could use any object I desired. My mother's personal belongings rapidly superseded the rough wood; the handle of a dressing-table mirror was one I often used, but my particular favourite was the oval-shaped lid of the silver urn in which my mother kept my father's ashes.

I got up now and went to splash some cold water over my face in the bathroom, but the pleasure of feeling cool was momentary. The instant I turned the tap off and dried my face my skin felt hot and clammy again.

I still felt tired too, as though I had had no sleep at all, and I sat down on the pale green tiles and leant my head against the wall. From the small bathroom window I could see the horizon which looked red like the edge of a distant planet. It reminded me of the cover of the book Serge was reading. It was called *The Perspex Planet* and the picture on the front was of a naked girl holding a ball of fire in the palm of her hand. Behind her you could see an outline of fire like an angel's halo. I stared out from the window over the city. There had been talk of forest fires reaching the suburbs and of the munitions factory and the chemical plants on the outskirts burning to the ground. The news broadcasts did not confirm these rumours, but at night we would be woken by the sound of fire engines screaming through the streets and we could all smell burning. I knew about fire and I knew its smell.

I heard a key turn somewhere along the corridor and the sound of footsteps walking down the central stairwell and then disappearing. It must be one of the many occupants of the building leaving for work. I went back to the bedroom where Serge lay and nestled up beside him.

'I had the strangest dream last night,' I whispered in his ear and Serge smiled drowsily in the way he did first thing in the morning. He always looked as though he'd walked across whole continents in his dreams.

'I told you you shouldn't eat cheese before going to sleep,' he said.

'It wasn't a bad dream, just strange.'

Serge was a good-looking man. He was dark and complete; the precise image of the man I wanted to be with. Before I met him I had been in a long relationship that had ended miserably. I was tired and withdrawn but Serge had changed all that. After I had finished with R—, I had gone to stay for the winter in the small spa town of Cauterets high up in the mountains. I went there to take the waters and relax. The pools were deep and dark and salty and lying in them helped me to forget. I would slip into the water and push myself down under the surface, totally submerging myself in the warm saline solution, and when I resurfaced I would lie quite still with eyes closed. All I could hear was the sound of my own breathing, a rasping boom in my ears, and I felt like a piece of driftwood afloat at sea and the feeling was one of great space and depth.

I read of a river once, called Lethe, a river of the underworld that to all those who drank of its waters caused an amnesia. These then were the waters of Lethe and within the river's folds I felt safe and at peace.

Sometimes I would sit by the side of the pools and watch the other bathers floating before me. Most of them were elderly men and women, their skin grey and wrinkled as though they had lain in the water for hundreds of years. I wondered if they too had come here to wash away their memories. I would pass them by and they would nod and smile at me in complicity.

I took the waters every day, leaving the small hotel at daybreak and walking the short distance to the building which housed the pools, down the quiet streets, past the central square. In the evenings, on my way back, I would stop off at a café to eat before returning to my room and lying down to read and sleep. I lived by this routine. I did not want to be noticed but enjoyed the invisibility of this existence.

The first night I had arrived in Cauterets I had turned up at the hotel very late and a young girl had come to the desk and given me a key. I had crept up the stairs and down the long corridor as quietly as I could, so as not to disturb the other guests, but my footsteps made the bare floorboards creak and as I reached my room the door to the one opposite opened and a thin old man had appeared in striped blue pyjamas.

'Do you ever wonder why floorboards creak?' he hissed.

I stopped and shook my head.

'Because of all the dead bodies. It's not floorboards that creak. It's the victims. You're waking the dead.'

'I'm sorry,' I said, but before I had time to finish my apology he had slammed his door fast behind him.

I had been in Cauterets three weeks before I met Serge. One evening as I approached the square I heard laughter and the sound of applause. A group of people were gathered round a troupe of circus performers. From a distance the arrangement looked like a magic circle: the spectators in shadow while a marvellous light glowed from the centre. I drew nearer. There was a knife-thrower, a young girl who charmed plastic snakes, a man with feather wings who walked on stilts, a one-armed woman who juggled ten silver balls on her feet, and a fire-eater. I stood and watched for a while as one by one the performers took their turn, and then the fire-eater stepped into the circle and immediately I was in awe. I watched as the man's hands threw the flames up into the air and how the people lifted their faces to see him make the fire dance in giant loops about his head.

I remember afterwards walking over to the café and sitting down at a table by the window. Although it was cold outside I ordered myself a drink filled with ice. The sight of the fire-eater swallowing the flames had made me thirsty. I stared out of the window for a time and then I remember turning round and looking across the café. The fire-eater was sitting at a table on the far side of the room, watching me.

It was Serge who joined me, although, as he always insists, it was I who first smiled at him. He came over to my table and asked if he could sit down.

'I saw you watching,' he said.

'There were a lot of people watching.'

'I know, but you're not from here, are you?'

I shook my head. 'No. I'm not from round here. I don't know how long I'll stay here.'

Serge lit a cigarette.

'Why fire?' I said. 'Why fire-eating?'

'Because fire is pure. It's not like other elements. Water and air. They are polluted. Not fire. To breathe fire is . . . Give me your hand,' he said.

He took my hand in his and turned it over, palm up, and stroked my skin with his fingers. Then he picked up my glass, took out a piece of ice and began very slowly to draw it over my skin. He rubbed it gently at first and then he pressed it into the centre of my palm until my skin hurt and all the while he stared into my eyes. When the ice had melted he drew his cigarette close to my skin.

'Can you feel it? The heat?'

'Of course,' I said and my hand flinched slightly.

He put the cigarette end closer still. Fingers of grey smoke curled around my wrist. The end of his cigarette was burning. I could see the red tip glowing while the smoke rose slowly upwards.

'Ice burns too,' he said.

'That's different. Fire is harsher.'

'Not really. Let me teach you to eat it. You wouldn't be afraid then.'

'My mother always told me it was dangerous to play with fire.'

'Not if you're taught properly.'

'I might get my fingers burnt.'

'What if I were to burn you now?' His clasp tightened suddenly, and instead of looking at me he stared down at the cigarette in his hand.

'Don't,' I said and in a moment he had released me. I placed my hand underneath the table.

'But it mesmerised you. Right?' he said. 'Just for a second you wanted it to burn you. Am I right?'

'No one wants that.'

'Maybe.' He threw his cigarette down on to the floor and put it out with his boot. 'All gone,' he said, smiling and raising his arms in playful submission.

We talked into the night and when the café closed we walked through the cold, empty streets of the town. Serge wrapped me up in his coat which trailed on the ground like a ballgown. Once we stopped at a shop window full of statues and lamps and plastic bottles in the shape of the Virgin Mary and he told me a story about a young boy he had seen pissing into one of these bottles as he stood behind some caravans at a fairground. Serge had worked in fairs and circuses all over the world and when he wasn't travelling he would perform on the streets of the city where he lived.

BRIE

When first light crept into the sky I gave back Serge's coat and he left me at the door to my hotel. I lay down on my bed and by the time I awoke the circus had departed.

I didn't believe I would see him again but shortly afterwards a postcard arrived. The painting on the front of the card was called *St George and the Dragon*, only there was a third person in the picture – a woman – and she had the dragon on a lead. There was no writing on the back but three days later I packed my bag and headed for the city on the postmark. I caught the bus that left Cauterets once a day to weave down the mountain into Lourdes, and from Lourdes the night train to the city. The train was full of pilgrims returning from their blessings and cures and I sat wedged between two fat Germans and their pale daughter who stared at me with watery eyes. Outside fields slipped by from daylight into dusk, each filled with varicoloured cattle. I closed my eyes and when I opened them again it was morning and the train had arrived.

It took me seventeen days to find Serge in the city. I wandered the streets searching every quarter where performers worked, visiting every fair and circus asking if anyone knew of him or could tell me where he was. Most people just shook their heads or turned away, and then finally, one afternoon, I found him in the Place St Jean sitting by the edge of a fountain where water spurted from the mouths of three fishes. He wasn't surprised to see me. He'd been expecting me, he said, and I believed him. I believed he knew I would come. It was myself I doubted.

After I found Serge, I found an apartment at the top of an old grey building over a hairdressing salon. A girl with a pink bouffant and one with a blackcurrant crew-cut smiled at us as we walked past the window and then through a door at the side of the building. The estate agent said the salon gave discounts to tenants. He led me up a stone stairwell to the fourth floor and opened the door of my apartment. Each room was large and empty. The first time I entered a pigeon flew down from the ceiling. The previous occupant had left a window open and the bird flew right past me. When it landed I saw that its foot was missing. There was nothing but a gnarled stump at the end of a thin leg and the estate agent quickly shooed the bird out of the window. Whoever had lived there before had stripped the apartment of everything except a bed and a stained wooden table. The estate agent made some apology for the state of the place but somehow I liked it like that. I liked the fact that it was empty and that birds flew in through the windows. At night you could hear the trains and the sound of people below in the street. Without curtains the room never grew dark.

I bought bookshelves, a small desk to write at and a blue velvet couch. The rest of the space remained empty. Serge kept his own apartment on the far side of the city in a modern development which we labelled the 'New World' as the buildings felt empty. Apart from the sky, there was no sign of nature, not a tree, not a plant, not a weed. Serge said he liked it that way but I hated staying there and gradually he transferred more and more of his belongings to my place.

About a month after I'd moved in Serge bought me a cake smothered in candles. He knocked on my door and when I opened it he stood there holding the cake on a plate high above his head.

'Close your eyes,' he said when I had sat down on the couch and blown the candles out.

I heard him cross the room and open the door again. Then he returned and when he told me I could I opened my eyes.

'I've bought you a present.'

'Where?'

'You have to find it.'

I stood up and looked in the drawers of my writing desk.

'Very cold,' he said.

I moved over to the window.

'Antarctic conditions.'

'Is it in this room?'

'Maybe.'

I walked through to the kitchen.

'Much warmer,' he said, following me in and standing by the table.

I looked round the room at the fridge and then at the cooker.

'The cooker,' I said quickly, opening the oven door. Inside sat a glass tank. I crouched down. 'It's a lizard.'

FERMENTATION

'A chameleon, to be precise. It changes colour according to its surroundings,' he said. 'Look, I've bought some blue card.'

We took the tank through to the living-room and put it on the floor. Serge propped the card up behind the tank and then we sat down on the couch and waited

'What do you think he feels when the background is blue?'

'Sad probably,' Serge said. 'Blue is sad.'

'Not when the sky is blue.'

The chameleon's dark eyes slowly opened and closed.

'What do I feed it on?'

'It's a he, and he eats insects.'

'Not fire?'

'He's lost his touch. He told me as much when I saw him in the shop. If I have time I might teach him.'

'Fireflies then?'

'Maybe.'

'Thank you for buying him.'

'I think we shouldn't watch him.' Serge stood up. 'He's a watched pot. Get your coat. We'll go out.'

We walked by the river and later we went and sat in a café. Serge ordered a plate of raw red chillies and a bottle of water which he poured into two glasses and then set them in the middle of the table between us.

'Baptism by fire,' he said.

'Baptism's for believers.'

'Then, as the cliché goes, believe in me. We're christening your new apartment.'

He picked up a chilli with his fingers and put it in his mouth. His eyes widened and as he swallowed he smiled.

'Your turn.'

'I'll stick to water, thanks,' I said, putting my hand out for one of the glasses, but he pushed it back.

'Just eat one,' he said, picking another up with his fingers. 'Eat one. It can't hurt you.'

'I don't want to.'

'You're afraid. Eat one. Go on. Eat.'

I picked a chilli up from the plate and together we put them into our mouths. I could feel my mouth smarting with pain and the tears as they ran down my cheeks. Serge put another in his mouth. He was crying too; we were laughing and crying and eating and everyone in the café was watching us. I took two to catch up.

The pain was unbearable but we kept eating and staring at each other and then at the glasses of water. Finally Serge grabbed at one. I sat back and watched him as he gulped the water down, letting it spill over his chin, and then he grabbed the second glass and drank that too. When he had finished I took the bottle, poured some more water and then picked up the glass and took a small sip. He stared at me across the table.

'Why do you do that?'

'What?'

'Pretend.'

I took another sip and then flung the rest of it over him.

'Baptism by water,' I said, and stood up to go.

Serge remained motionless for a moment and then began to laugh, the water dripping down his face.

I walked round the table, leant over him and began wiping the water off with a napkin. 'Everyone's watching us,' I said into his ear.

He got up and bowed to the audience.

When we returned we made love on the floor of the apartment with the chameleon sitting in his tank beside us.

'I'll pay you back for that,' Serge whispered as he pinned my arms down so that splinters of wood dug into my skin.

I turned my head away. The chameleon was watching us with his still, cold eyes.

'He's changed colour,' I said.

The first time we made love we were walking home through the ninth district. It was a few days after I had found Serge and we had been visiting some of his friends who lived by the station. After we left their apartment we walked for a time and then Serge ducked down a small side alley and motioned for me to follow him. This corridor, for that was all it was, a narrow passage leading from one street to another, smelt of piss and old men's excrement. Halfway down Serge stopped and opened a door. He led me into an empty building. When I looked up I could see thousands of stars through blackened beams. The building was completely gutted, nothing but a dry black shell.

Serge had prepared everything; paraffin and torches already lay in the centre of the room.

'Stand here,' he said as he led me to an open space near the back of the building.

He lit his torches and then began to walk around me throwing the flames into the air. I could feel the heat against my cold skin as the torches flew inches from my face. I could hear the fire as Serge threw it over my head or past my face and caught it and threw it and caught it again and my eyes became mesmerised by the flames and watching his hands as he caught each torch over and over. When he stopped he came and stood before me; stock still. He tilted his head far back and opened his mouth to eat the flames. He put the fire into his mouth and one by one the torches went out and we stood in the dark.

In general I cannot remember the first time I made love to my previous lovers. I remember particular things about each of them: Luke whose lips tasted of salt from the sea and Jan who liked to bind my hands with cord. Xavier caught my attention by diving underneath me as I swam past him in the local pool. I was in love with Jess for months before he noticed me, and then there was Ethan who took me walking along the railway tracks and fed me raspberries and Klaus in the snow, whose light blue eyes I still feel resting upon me. There was Mark who repaired TVs and liked to make love to old Frankenstein movies and when I kissed Ben I remember tasting oranges. But the moment I first made love to each of them blends into one slightly awkward unsatisfying memory that I have forgotten or reinvented to suit my mood. The truth of the moment is faint and remote, like books I have read where I remember parts of the plot but more often than not mix the storylines up or confuse fiction with fact.

With Serge it was different. I felt like an animal that has been caught in a car's headlights. He laid the torches down at my feet and easily drew me to him

At first when he pressed his body against mine I found the smell and the taste of him repugnant. He tasted of burnt skin and paraffin, like a man who has escaped a burning house or flown upwards from Hell. The smell caught in my throat and made my stomach heave. I wanted to draw back from him, but his grasp was too strong. He pushed me back against the wall and at first kissed my face gently, brushing my eyes and parting my lips with his tongue. Then slowly he knelt down at my feet, drawing his hands down the sides of my body, watching me watching him as he raised my skirt and kissed between my thighs. He slipped my underwear down and brushed his face against my sex and then slowly flicked his tongue against my lips, parting them and delving deep inside me. I could feel his hands caressing my buttocks and his finger working its way into the small firm hole. A spark of pleasure ran through my body. Serge could feel it too. I stood on the tips of my toes and his finger pushed deeper into me; I bent my knees slightly and his tongue flicked up into my sex. I could not escape but when I was at the point of coming he rose up and stood to face me, his eyes cast into mine like nets round a fish, and he turned me round and pushed my legs as wide apart as they would go. I could feel him stroking my sex, teasing me with his fingers, watching as my body responded to his touch, and then I felt his hardness pushing into me as my face scraped against the cold black wall and all the time he whispered my name into my ear and I could smell the smell of fire.

Afterwards we walked home in silence and Serge laid me down on the bed and bathed me with cottonwool dipped in warm water and oils. He washed me gently and kissed my arms and legs where I had cut them against the burnt-out walls and drawn blood and finally I fell into a deep sleep. I can't remember ever having slept so long or so soundly. Serge said it was the sleep of the neophyte and then he laughed and countered his statement. 'Or perhaps of the lost.'

BEAUMONT

A gentle, sweet, creamy cheese with a soft rosy rind and subtle flavour. Do not eat if distended or bitter.

'I feel sick,' I said.

'You want to be sick?'

'Yes. I'm going to throw up.'

Serge stepped out of the way just in time. I sat down on the pavement and vomited into the gutter.

Until the moment when the thin slip of paper turned from blue to pink we had simply been two people in love, and then I started to vomit. I sat in the bathroom on the rim of the bath and stared at the test result in disbelief. Serge knocked on the door to see if I was all right and I slipped the paper out to him.

'What's this?'

'It's a test result.'

'I don't understand,' he said and I unlocked the door and held out the packet for him to see.

'You're pregnant?'

'Yes.'

He stared at the paper and then turned it over as though looking for a message written in invisible ink.

'It's hardly a message from God. Are you sure? It looks blue to me. That's blue.'

'It's pink. I saw it change colour. That is not the colour it started out as. It's pink. That's why I've been feeling sick.'

Serge took a step towards me and as he did so he dropped the slip of paper and knelt down to retrieve it. When he stood up he took me by the hand and led me to the bedroom. He made love to me that morning more gently than he had ever done before and when we had finished I lifted the sheet up over my head.

'You look like an ivory moth,' he said as I brought the sheet down to rest over us.

Serge still wanted me to learn to eat fire. I allowed him to keep all his equipment in my apartment in a small kitchen cupboard under the sink. There he stashed bottles of paraffin and torches and sheets of old cotton which he'd tear into strips and bind round the torches.

'I still want to teach you,' he said more than once every week, usually when he was packing his stuff into his bag ready to go out. 'Tell me when you're ready. You'd love it,' he'd say, taking my face between his hands, brushing my skin with his fingers. 'Let me teach you. It's quite safe.'

'Why? I don't expect you to learn to write stories.'

'That's different. Fire-eating's not a job.'

'It frightens me,' I said. And I'd hold up my hands and

make as if my fingers has been burnt, putting them into my mouth to assuage the pain.

'Just imagine,' he'd say. 'A fire-eating pregnant woman. There haven't been many of those. In fact you'd probably be the first.'

'I'm feeling ill. I don't want to eat fire.'

He shrugged his shoulders and I could see he was hardly listening. He was looking at the pregnant woman and the acts she could perform.

'You'd be extraordinary,' he said.

'I'd be arrested. For roasting my child.'

'We could call her Joan of Arc.'

'She'd look like a pig on a spit and no man would want her,' I replied, but Serge shook his head.

'No,' he said. 'She would have flame-red hair and her eyes would dazzle anyone who dared look at her. She would dance circles of fire around all men who desired her.'

'Sounds as if you already do. Who is she?'

Serge looked at me and then turned to leave the room.

'I was teasing,' I said quickly. 'I love it that you want this child.'

'Sure you do,' he said.

'You do want this child?'

He stood on the far side of the room and looked at me for a time without speaking. I could rarely, if ever, tell what Serge was thinking. His eyes were dark and stared right through me. Sometimes I felt he made me disappear altogether.

'How can you ask that?'

'I just did.'

'And I just told you,' he said quickly.

Serge went out most days to work and I would sit at my desk and try to write. Sometimes he would leave early in the morning before I awoke and stay out till after I had fallen asleep. We missed whole days like that. It was hard to keep track and yet it didn't seem to matter. When I awoke on the second or third day of his absence, he would be eating in the kitchen or sitting in the living-room watching TV and it was as though he had always been there. He filled the gaps of his absence perfectly. He was always with me.

One night he came home after being away a few days. I was in bed asleep with the window open and the heat as my blanket. I felt Serge climbing into the bed and turning me over. He kissed my face and my neck and I could feel his hands brushing against my stomach and then all I could see were the child's baby-blue eyes. It was as though it were watching us, as though there was a third person present, and I pushed Serge away.

'I'm sorry.'

'What's the matter?' he said and put his hand out to touch me, but I pushed it away and Serge got up from the bed and went into the living-room. When he didn't return I went to find him, but he had fallen asleep on the couch. He was too tall to lie straight. His body was curled up like a child's, his head resting on the palm of his hand.

For a while I sat on the floor in the corner of the room and watched him sleeping. The lines of his face were lost in the shadows and he looked different somehow to the person I knew, a stranger in the dark of the room. At one point he opened his eyes and looked over to where I sat. He smiled at me in his sleep.

'I'm sorry,' I said but he had already closed his eyes.

The sickness persisted. I threw up in the mornings and in the afternoons and the smell of the vomit began to mingle with the smell of the rubbish wafting up from the streets.

'Try these,' Serge said one night when he returned home. He was carrying a small bag from which he took out three lemons. 'I've heard if you suck on a lemon when you want to be sick it stops the feeling.' Then he stood in the kitchen and started juggling them in his hands. 'Fresh lemonade's good too.'

'Who says?'

'I read it somewhere.'

'Do I smell?'

'A bit. After you've thrown up.'

'It's not attractive, is it?'

'Just try the lemons. They're supposed to help. I don't like seeing you ill.'

'You smell too sometimes.'

'I absolutely never smell,' he said, laughing and throwing the lemon across the room for me to catch.

'Maybe I'll learn to juggle.'

'You're throwing up enough as it is.'

'Very clever,' I said, and I chucked the lemons as hard as I could at his head, but each of them missed.

The next day when I went up to the markets I took one with me. I caught the Métro and sat in the carriage counting the stops and holding a lemon segment in my hand. The woman sitting opposite me was dressed in tight-fitting snake-skin trousers and a snake-skin top and as I looked at the strange green scales my vision became blurred round the edges and everything grew pale and watery. I held the lemon to my nose and then I sucked on it but its bitterness made me feel even worse and I tipped the contents of my bag out into my lap and then threw up in it full force. My vomit was salmon-coloured and when I had finished being sick I placed the lemon on top of it and then snapped the bag shut. The snake woman smiled at me.

'They never worked for me either,' she said, curling one long, virid leg round the other. 'Try a mint next time,' she said.

When it came to my stop I got off and dumped the bag in a bin. Outside in the markets I walked past animals: tanks full of locusts and fish and cages full of hens and rabbits that stank and looked sick. A large cage of white mice sat on a pile of crates. They scrabbled around in the sawdust and a man put his hand down and swung one up by its tail. He dangled it in the air and kissed it on the nose. Its eyes were pink and transparent like fish eggs. I walked on through the food stalls where the wasps were feeding. A small boy picked a plum up from under a stall and held it out to his mother.

'Don't eat,' I heard her say. 'There are maggots.'

People swatted at flies in their hair.

'It's disgusting,' the words were whispered again and again.

I found a cheese stall: a long table with a white cloth. The man had brought farm cheeses into the city to sell but everything was crawling with flies and I turned away and then I smelt the fire.

I walked through the crowd and shortly afterwards saw Serge and a small group of his friends gathered under a railway bridge chatting and drinking. I was about to walk over and join him. I recognised a couple of them: Boo the knife-thrower, who was dressed in an old Russian costume, and Stephane. There was a girl there too. She walked up to Serge. She was very young and pretty with red hair that fell in thick curls round her bare shoulders and I saw her put her arm around him and he bent down and kissed her. I watched as they both began unpacking his bag and preparing the bandages. She picked up one of the torches and wrapped a thin cotton strip around it and I saw Serge showing her how to wrap it so that it was just tight enough and then she took a drink from the bottle of paraffin and swirled the liquid round in her mouth like a fine wine before lighting the torch.

Serge stood behind her and lifted her arm and then I saw him direct her to spit over the flame and as she did so the flame roared out of her mouth and I stood there and watched. When she had finished she laid the torches down and turned around to face Serge and I saw that the right side of her face was completely disfigured. Serge put his hand out to her cheek and softly ran his fingers down the deeply scarred tissue. He bent down and blew on her skin and she laughed and he kissed her and I felt my whole stomach dip.

I took the Métro home and waited for Serge to come back. It didn't take long for him to return. He brought me a large bunch of eskimo roses.

'They smell good,' he said. 'Smell them.'

I put my face to the flowers.

'They're beautiful,' I said as he kissed me and then he laughed.

'You've got pollen on your nose. You look like a clown.'

I felt anger rise inside me as I went to the mirror in the hall and looked at my face smeared with gold dust.

Serge put his equipment down on the kitchen table and then went and had a shower. I listened to the sound of the water and when he had finished he came through to where I was sitting.

'Have you had a good day?'

'Yes,' he said, sitting down opposite me at the kitchen table and lighting a cigarette. 'Put them in water or they'll die.'

'Where were you?'

'Over by the markets.'

'Did you meet friends?'

'Yes,' he nodded. 'I was with friends.'

'Anyone I know?'

'Boo and Stephane.'

'Just Boo and Stephane?'

'A few others. Is this leading somewhere?'

'It's conversation,' I said. 'I just wondered if you were with any friend in particular.'

'I was with friends. Plural. Boo, Stephane, Justine.'

'Justine?'

'A friend.' Serge got up from the table and opened the fridge door. 'I'm hungry,' he said.

'Is she a special friend? Justine?'

'What is this?'

'I want to know what the word "friend" means exactly to you.' My voice was rising.

'Exactly?'

'Yes,' I said.

'Are you jealous? You *are* jealous. You're ridiculous,' he said, closing the fridge door gently and coming to stand behind me. 'Justine is a friend, that's all. I've known her since she was a child. She wants to learn to eat fire. She's always wanted to learn. You haven't.'

'What happened to her face?'

'Her face?'

'Yes, Serge. Her face. What happened to her pretty little face?'

'You've seen her?'

'Right.'

'When did you see her?'

'Today. What happened to her face?'

'She's always liked fire.'

'And you like teaching her?'

'Yes, I like it. I like teaching her. I like passing on my skills. You've never wanted to learn.'

'I don't want to learn, so you screw someone else? Is that it? Is that what's going on?'

'You've lost me.'

'I saw you kiss her.'

Serge began to massage my neck. 'Try and relax. She's a friend. There's nothing between Justine and me. You're imagining where there is nothing to imagine. You're tired,' he said, leaning down and kissing me.

He smelt wet and soapy and part of me wanted to turn round and wrap my arms around him. To kiss him because I believed him.

'Was the accident your fault?'

'Is that what you think?'

'Well, was it? Did you burn her? Did she scream out in pain and now you feel guilty and that's why you sleep with her?'

'Stop it,' Serge said. 'These questions are stupid.' He was continuing to massage my neck and I thought I could feel his grip becoming tighter. 'You're tired. Justine is a friend.'

'Stop touching me,' I said and then I turned round and caught his face with my nails.

BEAUMONT

Serge put his hand up to the blood.

'I'm sorry.' I whispered the words in the silence.

'You're ridiculous.'

He grabbed me by the hair and pulled my head back as far as it would go until I was gasping for air like a fish.

'Let's see how green your skin is,' he said, bending down close to me so I could feel the warmth of his breath on my face. 'It's seeping right through you,' he said and then with one hand he picked up a bottle of paraffin that sat on the table.

'You're hurting.'

'No I'm not. I'm going to teach you something.'

He forced the bottle between my lips and made me drink the liquid. It tasted strong and oily, like the idea of taking petrol into your mouth, and I thought I would vomit and then he forced my head down to the floor and told me to spit. He picked up a torch from the table and held it lengthways between his teeth, and still holding my head by the hair he lit a match and set light to the torch. He pulled me from the kitchen into the living-room and threw me down on the sofa, leaning his whole weight against me, holding my head back over the arm of the sofa as though I were in a dentist's chair, and then very slowly he began lowering the torch down towards my face. I could feel the warmth of the flames.

'If you struggle, you get burnt,' he said. 'That's the rule, so open your mouth and open it wide or you'll end up looking just like Justine.'

I did as he said, all the time thinking of the skin on the

young girl's face and the way Serge had caressed it so gently. I *was* jealous of his touch and for a moment I wanted the flames to come closer, to burn me. My head ached where Serge was pulling at my hair.

'Now you are going to swallow,' he said. He pushed the burning torch closer to my face and then away and then closer and finally he put the whole of the torch into my mouth and I could feel myself burning and choking. 'Close your mouth,' I heard his voice shouting and I closed it against the flames and when I opened it again I breathed out, and fire leapt from within me. I was breathing out fire that leapt in the air and then there was absolute silence.

Serge released his grip and leant down and put his mouth to mine. He touched my lips with his tongue and kissed me and then he threw me back against the couch like some discarded piece of rubbish.

'You're mad,' I screamed. 'You could have set fire to everything. You could have killed us both. You're mad.'

'Us both? Is that you and the baby, or you and me?'

'Now who's jealous? Now whose skin's fucking green?' I felt the room beginning to spin around me and I put my head down between my legs. 'I think I'm going to be sick.'

'Try a lemon.'

'They're too fucking bitter.'

'You should know,' he said, walking towards the door.

Moments later he was gone. I thought he would slam

the door behind him but instead he left it open and I sat and stared out into the dark corridor listening to the echo of his steps growing fainter and fainter.

When I heard the door to the building close I got up and followed. I ran down the stairs and out into the street. Serge was only a little way ahead of me and it didn't take me long to catch him up. He knew I was behind him and then I was by his side walking in step but he didn't look at me. He just kept walking, his hands deep in his pockets, and eventually I stood still on the pavement and watched as he disappeared round the corner. I stood like that for several minutes. I felt someone push past me. I thought, if I walk round the corner Serge will be standing there waiting for me. All I need do is walk a few steps further and look round the corner. He will be standing there waiting for me. I walked slowly and when I came to the corner I stood and looked at all the people passing by.

I went back to the apartment and sank down on the floor and wept in the silence.

Serge did not return to the apartment that evening. I had to take a long shower to wash away the black smudges from my face and arms and to scrub out my mouth which tasted of ashes. Afterwards I cleared away the torches and mopped up the floor where I had spat out the paraffin and then I prepared some food: a large panful of macaroni cheese made with some cream cheese that was left in the fridge. It was comfort food; a dish my mother used to serve when I was sick as a child. My body could not seem to decide between hunger or nausea. At one moment I would want to throw up and in the next eat without pause.

After I had finished my meal I went and sat by the window. I thought I might glimpse Serge standing in the street or walking towards the building but he didn't appear. The apartment seemed more empty than it had ever been before when Serge had left. I went to the wardrobe in the bedroom, took down a green shirt that belonged to him and pressed it to my face. It smelt of him, his sweat and the smoke and the paraffin, and I pushed my hands deep down into the empty sleeves and then curled up on the bed and fell asleep.

As he watched from a chair in the corner of the room I ran my fingers along a line of eggs that were arranged in order of size on a table. There were tiny quails' eggs and hens' eggs and speckled ducks' eggs but my fingers stopped when I reached a large white goose egg that lay at the end of the row dwarfing all the others. I picked this egg up and then went and lay down on the bed under the window. I rolled the thick oval shell between my hands, down the middle of my stomach and between my legs before finally lifting it and cracking the shell into two halves on the window ledge and then letting its heavy golden centre fall on to my stomach.

'Come here,' I said and he approached the bed and

stood over me and stared down at the yolk that lay quivering on my skin like a huge yellow eye. I held my hand out to him and he climbed on top of me and lowered himself down to meet me, all the while being careful not to touch the egg, not to let skin touch skin. He kissed my eyes and my lips and my neck, holding his weight on his arms, aware of the yolk that lay between us.

His mouth was soft and his saliva sweet. He ran the tip of his tongue from my mouth down my neck to my dark full nipples and I rose beneath him as he encircled them, turning them hard. I wanted to crush the yolk against his skin but he held me down, putting the full weight of his body against my wrists so that I found it difficult to move, and then he sucked on my breasts, gently clasping my nipples between his teeth and drinking from the skin. His tongue slipped down my body to where the yolk lay whole and complete, a perfect sack of thick rich liquid that rested on my soft belly ready to split and spill.

Carefully he opened my legs and brushed his hand against the soft velvet creaminess of my sex. He pushed against me, his sex against mine, and I felt my whole being open out towards him as he gently pushed himself inside me, all the time holding himself back from touching the eye of my stomach. I knew he wanted to shove himself against me, to ram himself deep inside my flesh, but he couldn't allow this. The yolk lay between us, staring upwards, like the pressure of a long-held promise, and I was forcing him to take his pleasure with a measured, almost detached precision.

When he came, he held me down firmly until I could feel the muscles in his arms and legs relax and then he carefully let go of my wrists, which were white where he had clasped them, and pushed himself up.

'Now eat it,' I whispered into his ear and put my hand on his head and forced his face down to my stomach. 'Eat it,' I said as his whole body tried to resist me. He looked at me and then he wrapped his mouth around the warm yellow yolk and sucked the whole from my stomach. The skin broke in his mouth and thick yellowy liquid spilled from his lips.

When I awoke Serge's shirt was twisted tightly around me and in the heat of the night it was wet with sweat. I could see the lizard sitting in its tank where Serge had placed it at the foot of the bed. It was quite motionless and it was staring straight at me with its cold dark eyes. I tried to close mine, but each time I did so all I could see was Serge lying next to Justine, kissing her softly on the scarred side of her face. The lizard's tongue flicked out in the dark.

I got up. In the apartments opposite people had dragged their mattresses on to the balconies and lay on their backs with their eyes to the sky. I could see their dark outlines, lying stacked like refugees under the hot moon. Madame R– (Serge and I had named all these characters) was sitting in her armchair by the open window fanning herself with her husband's newspaper and I could see Doc, who lived directly opposite me, sitting up in bed reading one of his medical books. There was no privacy in the heat of night. What would otherwise remain firmly closed was opened for the world to see. Carlotta returned from work a little after four am. She took off her blonde wig to wipe away the sweat and lit a cigarette. Sometimes she would take her clients up to her flat and Serge and I would sit at my window and watch the dimly lit shadows which their bodies cast against the walls, but usually she worked on the streets. 'She probably prefers it like that,' Serge said. 'There's no intimacy on the street.' That night I watched as she smoked her cigarette in the dark and then stretched out on the balcony.

No one could sleep in this heat which made everyone drowsy. Instead we were all day-dreaming of cool nights, between cool sheets. Everyone was dreaming of sleep.

I sat up like this until dawn. Everything was hazy in the early-morning sun as though someone had sketched the buildings over parchment. Three small sparrows were dusting themselves at the base of a tree below. The earth appeared to crumble at the slightest touch of their wings. The city was returning to dust.

PROCESSED CHEESE

Processed cheese is usually made with pasteurised milk. It possesses little taste, less aroma and is most often flaccid. If at all possible, it is to be avoided. Never serve at dinner parties.

Serge returned a few days later. I had been out to look for him in all the places he usually frequented but I hadn't seen him. I saw Justine instead. I came across her sitting in a café. Part of me thought I should simply walk by, but then I found myself taking a table in the corner where I had a good view of her. I liked the idea that she didn't know me, had never met me, and therefore couldn't see me. For all I knew Serge had never told her about me and I didn't exist at all.

Her face fascinated me. I wanted to reach out and touch it. You could see where the veins had risen on the shiny pulled skin and how her mouth was slightly twisted where the flames had eaten into the muscle.

'How did that happen?' I would casually ask her one day. I would be a nosey passer-by, or a plastic surgeon offering hope of a miracle skin graft.

'I am learning to eat fire. My teacher. He was demonstrating how to breathe out the flames and the flames caught my face.'

'But that's terrible.'

'Not really. It's brought us closer together. It was an accident, but he likes the scars,' she'd say.

I watched as she gently tugged her long red hair and pulled it over her cheek to hide her scars. She drank her coffee and read from a book and eventually she paid her bill and left. I had thought of following her, to see if she led me to Serge, but something inside stopped me.

On my way back home I stopped off and bought some fruit and vegetables at a market by the river and then walked through the streets to the apartment. The girl with the blackcurrant crew-cut was sitting on a sofa outside the salon. She was wearing a dress the colour of lemon curd and drinking a purply-blue drink out of a glass filled with ice.

She smiled as I walked by. 'You live upstairs, don't you?' she asked.

'Yes I do.'

'Ever thought of having a haircut?'

'Not really. I've thought of having it dyed, though.'

'What colour? We have lots of colour charts. Our speciality is dyeing,' she said, pouring some of the strange purple liquid into a second glass and handing it to me.

'Red.'

'Really? Red?'

'Yes. What's wrong with red?' I said, sitting down next to her on the sofa and sipping the drink.

'It's grape juice,' she said. 'You just don't strike me as a red person. I had you down as a secret blonde. Ask yourself this. Do you have a lot of red in your wardrobe? Does red complement your skin tone? Is your personality red? Do you like red meat? Do you eat a lot of red vegetables? Do you wait for a red light before you cross a road? These are questions you should consider.'

'Yes,' I said. 'I see.'

'Do you see red a lot? That is a very important question. I myself am a mixture of blue and red,' she put her hand to her head. 'Five days out of seven I feel very blue and then every now and then I see deep red. Those days are very ugly. But you see, don't you – purple is my colour.'

'I see red a lot,' I said.

'Are you pregnant?'

'What's that got to do with it?'

'Are you?'

'I'm pregnant, yes.'

'Are you exercising?'

I shook my head.

'Come inside, I want you to meet someone.'

She stood up and put down her drink and I followed her inside the shop. The girl with the bouffant was combing through someone's hair.

'This is Peggy,' the blackcurrant girl said. 'And my name is Rachel. Peggy teaches yoga. She'll show you some good exercises.'

Rachel turned to Peggy and relieved her of the comb and then Peggy took a pillow off one of the chairs and put it on the floor.

'Lie down with your head on the pillow,' she said, beaming at me and kneeling down on the floor. 'I'll show you something that isn't very strenuous. Close your eyes. Now keep your body relaxed and breathe in and out so that you are aware of your breathing. Contract your thigh muscles as hard as you can. Hold that tension and slowly release it. Now tighten your stomach muscles. Hold the tension and slowly release it. Do the same with the muscles all over your body. One by one tighten them and then slowly release the tension. Let your body flow. Let your body open out. Feel the tension slipping from your shoulder blades. Let your thoughts drift away and your breathing control you. Feel lightness and sweetness enter your body at every breath and when you exhale feel the poison leaving your body. Your body is soft. Your skin is like silk. Open your body out. Spread your limbs out.'

I lay on the floor listening to Peggy's voice and feeling myself slowly drifting away. I was a giant cheese and my body was spreading and oozing out like an over-ripe Camembert on a large white plate. When I opened my eyes again Peggy and Rachel were standing over me smiling. The woman whose hair Rachel had been combing was still sitting in her chair. She was watching me too.

'How do you feel?' Rachel said.

'Great. Thank you.'

'Come down any time,' Peggy said. 'I could show you the cat position and a few others which are good for pregnant women.'

PROCESSED CHEESE

As I left the salon Rachel came to the door.

'I still think blonde,' she said. 'Red's a bit cheap.'

'You're right,' I said.

I walked slowly up the stairway to my apartment. I could feel almost immediately that Serge had been there some time before me, as surely as if a ghost had passed through my body, and when I entered the apartment I saw him standing by the window in the dark.

'You came back,' I said as he turned round. 'It's good to see you.'

'You too.' He bent his head slightly.

'You look tired.'

Serge nodded. 'Yes,' he said. 'I am tired.'

'Are you staying? Are you hungry?'

'No. I'm not staying. I'm going to go.'

'To Justine?'

'Don't do that.'

'I'm sorry. Are you hungry?'

I switched the light on in the kitchen and put the bag on the table and began to unpack some of the vegetables. 'I've got salad and things,' I said as I began washing tomatoes and lettuce in the sink and then I felt his arms wrap round my waist. His face brushed against my neck. 'I've missed you,' I said. He kissed my neck gently. 'I'm sorry. About Justine. I'm getting muddled,' I said. His hands turned me round to face him and he kissed me again and then stared at me.

'Listen, I'm going away for a while. Stephane has a job in Geneva. They need a fire-eater and I said I'd go.'

'Would you have left me a note?'

Serge put his hand in his pocket and drew out a small scrap of paper. On it he had scribbled: 'I'm leaving for Geneva tonight. They eat cheese there for breakfast! Back soon. Love Serge.'

'It was good of you to write.'

'Sarcasm doesn't suit you.'

'No,' I said. 'You're right. Your stuff's in the cupboard, I'll see you when you get back.'

'I was waiting for you, you know. I wanted to see you.'

'You'd better go.'

'Yes,' he said. I started to talk again but he held up his hand. 'I'll see you soon. Okay? Will you be okay?'

'I'll be fine. Thanks for waiting.'

I managed to walk past him and into the bedroom where I lay down on the bed. On the far wall was a large mirror with a photograph that a friend had taken of the two of us stuck into the frame. We were standing outside the gates at Versailles and Serge was laughing and making a chopping movement with his hand. I lay on the bed staring at the image while my body slowly drifted away.

Later, after he had gone, I got up and sat on the couch in the living-room. A packet of his cigarettes was stuffed down the sofa back. I took one out and lit it and then held the burning end to the back of my hand. I held it close so that it burnt the tiny fair hairs on my skin. The heat tickled me and then I turned my hand over and quickly stubbed the cigarette hard into my palm. For an instant there was no pain and then it was excruciating but I kept the cigarette there, grinding it down to a pulp until tears were pouring down my face, and I ran to the kitchen and held my hand under the cold-water tap. Every time I took it away from the water the pain returned and eventually I made myself an ice-pack and sat on the couch pressing it to my skin. By morning a watery blister had formed. It took several weeks for the wound to heal and when it did the skin was a different texture. It was a small shiny disk, like a vaccination scar. I would touch it occasionally. It made me feel sick.

My craving for cheese increased. One night at around twelve o'clock, desperate to eat, I was forced to go out on a shopping expedition to the late-night store between rue Marais and rue Bec. I didn't want to move. The heat had made me lethargic but I desperately wanted to assuage my hunger.

Outside the red machines were washing the streets in vain. The water slaked the pavements, dampening the dust and trickling down into the gutters between the piles of festering rubbish. There were several late-night bars still open with people sitting outside. A green light from a pharmacy display lit their faces, making them look as sick as the smell of the rubbish that lay mouldering around them. The stench was overpowering. It stung my nostrils and caught at the back of my throat. You could hear the flies and wasps as they swarmed in the warm night air and crawled over the piles, hatching in their millions in the blood of sanitary towels and remains of chopped liver.

I walked quickly down the centre of the road.

The owner of the shop nodded at me as I entered, then held his fingers over his nose and raised his eyes to the ceiling. His fingers were pudgy, like fat little puppy dogs. I could see his wife in the small front room that adjoined the shop. She was large also and rarely seemed to move from her armchair. Sometimes when she waddled through to serve, you could smell the smell of sweat through her thick nylon dresses.

The only cheese I could lay my hands on in the refrigerated section of the late-night store was a small packet of the processed kind. I lingered for a while in front of the unit, trying to benefit from the cooler air it cast off. Eventually I returned to the counter.

'Not much of a choice.'

'No deliveries,' the man said. 'If it continues like this . . .' and he raised his shoulders.

I bought the cheese and returned home.

The cheese was exactly 10cm by 10cm in size and came wrapped in thick, see-through plastic. There were six slices in the packet which I cut open with a pair of nail scissors, holding it up to smell its contents but there was absolutely no aroma. Each slice was thick and pale. I cut some bread and put two slices of cheese on top and then toasted it and took the plate to my bedroom where I sat with it on the bed and watched soap operas on TV.

PROCESSED CHEESE

Afterwards The Falling Joys came on and sang 'XYZ' and I went to sleep.

I had no dreams that night, or at least none I could remember once I had awoken, and I felt disappointed, empty almost, as though I had been cheated.

I went into the living-room and sat down on the couch and began drawing little sketches of pregnant animals: elephants and spiders and matchstick women with huge pieces of cheese inside their stomachs. My favourite was a picture of a mouse with six BabyBel lined up in its tummy like peas in a pod.

Later I took a shower and then went and stood in front of the full-length mirror in the bedroom. As a child I had rarely looked at myself in the mirror, or, if I did look, I never questioned the child that stared back. I took it for granted that it was me who stood there and hardly gave myself a second glance. Now I stared at myself but I hardly recognised the Siamese figure before me. My breasts were growing larger. My whole being was changing shape, transforming itself to accommodate the child within. I remembered a short film I had seen of a caterpillar turning into a butterfly and thinking how compact the chrysalis was and of the creature tightly packed inside. The molecules changed and re-formed themselves into bright shining wings and finally the camera showed the chrysalis split and the beautiful creature emerging and spreading its wings.

I ran my hand over my stomach. My skin was as smooth and expectant as a sealed envelope. I thought of

FERMENTATION

Serge sitting in some foreign city far away from me. I missed him; I missed hearing his voice and feeling his arms wrapped around me and his body close to mine. At times I wanted to write to him; I wanted to tell him about the heat. How it had grown steadily closer and how I could hardly breathe. I wanted to tell him that the city was returning to dust and would soon fall apart. Serge was in a place where there were cool breezes and the earth was green and fresh. He was breathing sweet air. I wondered if he would recognise me now. I stared at my face and the longer I stared the more distant I grew, like the photographs my mother kept of me as a child. I knew they were me and yet somehow they made no sense. I had disappeared.

When I went for my walk I waved at Peggy and Rachel through their window. Rachel was settling an old lady down under a dryer and Peggy was sticking plastic roses in her pink bouffant.

The sun shimmered on the pavement and the air was hot and hazy; the world outside my door was nothing but a mirage. An old woman crossed the street and asked me for some change. She held out her dirty hand and I gave her a few francs before she shuffled away.

PARMIGIANO REGGIANO

A medium- to strong-flavoured cheese with a distinctly sharp flavour. Works well as a dessert cheese served with pears, melon or figs. Initially its texture is hard but this is swiftly replaced by a wonderful melt-in-the-mouth quality. Sample the cheese before purchasing. If the taste does not linger or disappears too quickly, the cheese is not fully ripened.

I tried to take a walk every day now. Sometimes I would only get as far as the bar on the corner, where I would stay and watch the TV, but usually I tried to reach the public gardens to sit under what was left of the trees. I would watch the passers-by in their paper-thin clothes, their legs and arms visible, their skin pink and sticky with sweat. I could smell their skin burning under the sun and I would undress them as they paraded in front of me, releasing them from the burden of their clothing. I unbuttoned their shirts and slipped off their dresses and skirts and trousers and laid them down in my mind on the dry hard ground while they walked on oblivious. Everyone walked on by as I sat, quite still, on the park bench under the trees, changing shape in front of them, an invisible miracle, while their eyes were raised to the sky waiting and praying for the first fingers of rain.

I also took to visiting churches and the city's many museums. There was one in particular, a small museum on a narrow road off one of the main squares, which was always cool after the heat of the streets. I liked to walk

FERMENTATION

across its polished wooden floors between the marble figures. Each part of the museum was hung with gilt mirrors, presenting room after room of illusionary space. It intrigued me how something as simple as sand could perform the magic of reflection and my reflection always appeared to be cool, as though I were floating in water.

That day was different, though. That day I headed in the opposite direction, over the Pont Rochelle. The river was low; all the detritus that usually sank in its depths or was washed out to sea now floated to the top of the slow, shallow waters, a huge slick of greeny black effluence. And anything that didn't float stuck to the riverbanks, matted together with river weed like huge hairballs from a sick cat's stomach. As a child I had loved to wander along the dirty rim of the sea, scuffing my shoes against the rubbish that had washed up with the tides: the old boots, a doll's head, a car tyre, once even a computer terminal whose glass had been smashed out and which was crawling with fat pink butterfly crabs. I would make my way along this marine aisle with my mother's shopping basket hung over my arm, picking out violet sea urchins and long thin razor-shells. I loved their shapes, their creamy interiors and iridescent inner chambers; ice-blue whelks and baby starfish, fluted argonauts and green-lipped mussels. My mother had given me a conch shell for my tenth birthday. She said I would always be able to hear the sea as long as I kept the shell. I still have it now. It sits by my bed.

I crossed over the bridge as quickly as I could and on

the far side walked along the shaded boulevard of chestnut trees. Presently I came to a turning on my right and took one of the cobbled streets that led me down towards the markets. My destination was an old shop I could vaguely remember seeing on a previous walk through this quarter of the city. I continued to wander through the twist of the streets, trying to recall its precise location, until finally, more by chance than good memory, my goal appeared before me. It was a specialist cheese shop called, appropriately enough, Le Fromage.

A small silver bell rang as I pushed open the door. It was cool and dark inside and the first thing that hit me was the mossy aroma of the cheese which instantaneously made my mouth water. The line of customers moved slowly. They filed past the shining glass counters which were piled high with huge cheeses of all different shapes, sizes and colours. There were firm cheeses with deep-green veins and large round buttery cheeses that slowly oozed out on to plates. There were giant domes of cheese with orangey rinds and creamy pale cheeses that looked as though they had been rolled in black pepper. Waxy Edams and bloomy Bries were piled next to close-packed rows of blues. Some of the cheeses were bedded in straw while others lay on thick green leaves and were studded with walnuts. They came from all over the world, from Switzerland and Italy and France and China. The owner had arranged them alphabetically, according to country, so that they were positioned from East by the door, to West by the till. There were small white cards pinned onto each of the cheeses with their names written in black: Raveggiolo, Cheddar, Jizrael, Petit Bessay.

Behind the counter stood two boys and a girl, none of whom seemed older than twenty or so. The girl and one of the boys had the complexion of Brie and their hands looked pale also. But it was the second boy who caught my attention almost immediately. He was albino and it was hard not to stare at his eyes, which were absolutely pink, and his snow-white hair. Each of them wore a fresh white apron and each of them served the customers methodically in turn, but it was the albino to whom everyone looked. And then an older man appeared behind them. He didn't wear an apron and he stood with his hands behind his back smiling around the shop. There was something silvery about his appearance. He nodded at certain customers and served only occasionally. He seemed to choose his customers and it soon became apparent that it was he who owned the shop. I listened while he advised a young woman in front of me on the type of cheese she should serve at a dinner party she was giving. She explained that the main dish was to be salmon poached in vermouth.

'A dry white with the fish and a medium-to-mild cheese to follow would be appropriate,' he said, almost whispering his words into her ear.

She nodded appreciatively and he took down a small square cheese from a shelf behind him to let her taste. I could tell she was entranced and when she came to pick up the neatly wrapped package she smiled at him and I knew that smile.

When it was my turn, the albino was serving. His skin was white and pink like strawberries dipped in milk. I asked for something that was not too mild or too strong.

'I feel like something that will complement fruit,' I said, and the boy with the smooth, pale skin said, 'This came in just this morning.' He pointed to a huge cylindrical drum of cheese and then tapped on it with his fingers.

'Parmigiano Reggiano,' he said triumphantly, taking a wire device from under the counter. He pulled the wire taut and then carefully spliced the cheese open, revealing a wonderful, caramel-coloured granular paste. 'Come closer,' he said and I leant forward. 'Can you see?' There on the surface shone a film of moisture like sweat.

He slid his knife through a damp cloth and then gouged out a small piece which he offered me on the edge of the blade. The cheese tasted sweet with a slight pear-like bloom. I watched as he took a morsel and nibbled on it too.

'It's good?' he said.

'Yes, it tastes good.'

'About this much then?' he asked, indicating with the sharp metal edge just where he would cut.

I nodded. He weighed the cheese, wrapped the piece in a square of greaseproof paper, then slipped the whole into a blue and white striped bag.

It was only after I had made my purchase that the old gentleman spoke to me.

FERMENTATION

'You haven't been in here before, have you?' he asked timidly.

'No,' I said, taking the package from the counter.

'What is it you have bought?'

'Parmigiano.'

'A beautiful cheese. A beautiful cheese,' he said quickly and then continued to talk to me in a low, almost urgent voice. 'The way most people treat cheese is criminal. They plan their meal as carefully as a murderer plots the perfect crime, but they always forget about the cheese so then they trot off to the nearest supermarket and buy anything that's on offer – just like the murderer returning to the scene of the crime because he's forgotten something vital. That's when he makes his mistake. That's when he's caught out. Cheese should never be an afterthought. That's very important. Do you understand?'

I nodded my head.

'There is an old English rhyme which I forget in its entirety, but the main points are simple. Cheese should not be too salty like Lot's wife, nor too full of eyes like Argus. Never buy cheese that weeps like Mary Magdalen because that means it is full of whey, nor cheese that is hairy like Esau. These are good guidelines, don't you agree?'

'I'll remember,' I said.

'This Parmigiano comes straight from Italy, from the banks of the Po. It is just the right time of year for a good Parmigiano. It was sweet, wasn't it?'

'Yes, it tasted of pears.'

'What you tasted was the fullness of summer. It's the flavour of fruit and grass and flowers under the sun that gives cheese its true taste. Buttercups and pears, gentians and plums, sweet pink clover and tender green grass.' The old man put his hands together like a child and then spread out his fingers like a flower in bloom or a seashell opening in the warm tides of spring. 'It is alchemy. Chemistry at its finest,' he said. 'First the cow turns the grass into milk. A miracle. Then the milk is transformed. Golden cheese from pure white milk. You have to admit?'

I smiled. 'Yes. A miracle.'

'Of course,' he said, 'no two fields will yield the same crop. It is the earth and the minerals that truly define a cheese's flavour. One farmer I know grazes his cattle in an old graveyard. He swears that the grass that grows there is the richest in the area, and his milk does produce one of the sweetest cream cheeses I have ever tasted.'

The old man stopped talking. Then he made a little bow to me and turned away and I took this as my signal to leave.

Outside the shop I put the package into my basket and then walked slowly over to the City Library. A few people sat at the dark oak desks fanning themselves with magazines; an old woman slept in one corner. I thought I saw Serge disappearing behind one of the shelves, but when I followed him it turned out to be a much older man who didn't look like Serge in the slightest and I felt disappointed. It was as though Serge could appear to me at any time he wished and then disappear again. It was what he did when he lived with me. Now the same thing was happening after he had left. He kept reappearing. I'd see him walking down a street, crossing the park, sitting in a café, but each time I looked again it turned out to be a stranger and I'd miss him twice, three times as much.

I walked over to the Food and Cookery section which was situated on two shelves at the back of the library. The selection was scant. There were a couple of dog-eared books on cooking with woks, several volumes of a series called *The Fantasti-chef*, a book entitled *Success with Soups, Soufflés and Salads* and one or two cookery books for children with pictures of ginger men and jellies on the front. Tucked in between the aforementioned and a misplaced copy of *A Tale of Two Cities* was a tiny volume with the title *Cheese Lover's Handbook – A Complete Guide*. I took this book and then went and found a couple on pregnancy. The woman at the desk stamped them out for one month and I put them in my basket alongside the cheese.

When I returned home I sat down at my desk and opened my book at the page which referred to Parmigiano Reggiano. The book described the cheese in detail. It talked of the cheese-making process, using words such as 'skimming' and 'coagulation', and then of cauldrons and vats and infusing the cheese with rare moulds and salting it. By the time I had finished reading, my mouth was salivating and I knew I couldn't wait until supper to taste the Parmigiano. I cut three large slices and began greedily to eat. The cheese was rich and tasted fruity on my tongue.

It was night-time and I was travelling on the Métro. I believe I had been travelling for some time. The stations, which blurred past like glass tubes of neon, seemed familiar. So too did the people who stood on the platforms and stared in at the windows.

I sat smiling at all the beautiful passengers in my carriage and then a man came over to where I sat, leant down so his face was close to mine. He whispered gently in my ear.

Some time later I found that we were walking back to a house he said he owned in the suburbs.

When we arrived he showed me his room which was empty apart from a bed and various items of clothing scattered carelessly over the floor. I felt comfortable in this room. It smelt of new paint and wasn't cluttered with furniture or ornaments. I lay back on the soft downy bed and watched as the man took off his coat and draped it over the door. 'I'll be back in a minute,' he said and disappeared. I undressed and lay back down on the bed waiting for him to return. The house was very quiet. I thought I might detect the sound of running water or his footsteps down the corridor but, much as I strained to hear, the house was silent. When he didn't return I got up and went in search of him. The living-room and

FERMENTATION

kitchen and bathroom were all empty. Presently I saw a dim light showing under a door at the far end of the main corridor. I turned the handle and very slowly pushed the door open. In the half-light thrown from candles scattered about the room, I saw a young girl, completely naked, squatting on her knees on a bed in the centre of the room, her hands tied to the bedposts and a piece of white cloth tied around her eyes. The man who had brought me here stood over her, roughly brushing a blue silk scarf between her thighs. For a moment I watched transfixed as the young girl's back rose and fell, the muscles in her body tensing at the pleasure of feeling the soft silk rubbing against her. I could almost see how moist and dark the lips of her sex were and how open to the touch of the silk. 'Come and join us,' the man said and at the sound of his voice the blindfolded girl lifted her head in my direction. 'You can sit over here and learn,' he said, indicating a chair near the bottom of the bed. I sat down and watched as the man continued to brush the cool blue silk over the young girl's sex and the young girl's body arched and fell in a hypnotic movement. I could feel my sex growing wet and an excitement enveloped me. Part of me wanted to be the girl and part of me wanted to be the man. I wanted to be the man and place my hands on the young girl's hips and feel the movement of her body as it rose and fell. I wanted to be the girl and feel the touch of the silk as it was drawn over and over across my sex.

I got up and crouched down by the side of the bed to

watch more closely. I could see small beads of perspiration had formed on the girl's white thighs and I leant my head closer and began to lick her skin, tasting the salt of her body, and then the man stopped what he was doing and drew me up on to the bed. I knew what I needed to do. I was thirsty and I bent my head down and began to drink of the young girl's sweet juices, lapping at her dark sex like I would suck over-ripe fruit, and as I sucked I could feel my own sex swelling. And then I felt it, the raw silk being placed between my legs, and the man began to draw it over me, gently at first and then rougher, and my whole body felt as though it were collapsing inwards, folding in and melting through my sex which throbbed like a precious ruby. My tongue dug deep into the girl, straining now for every last drop of her juices, and her body writhed in a frenzy. I could see when I lifted my head that her wrists were covered in blood where she had pulled against the ties that bound her. I drank again, this time digging my fingers into the girl's flesh, tracing and imprinting my desire on her skin, until finally I felt the silk being withdrawn from between my legs and immediately I lay down on the bed exhausted and closed my eyes.

When I re-opened my eyes light was streaming in through the windows. I looked about me, blinking at the sun. The girl was no longer lying on the bed and the room was empty. I stood up and went back to the room where I had undressed the night before. My clothes lay on the bed just as I had left them. Once I had dressed I walked through the house trying to locate both the man and the girl, but everywhere I looked confirmed my fear that not only were they not there but that the whole house was empty. There was no sign that anyone lived there at all. No ornaments, no clothes in the wardrobe or towels in the bathroom. It was a shell: a house, perhaps, that no one had ever lived in.

The previous night we had entered through the back door and this was the door I chose to leave by. It closed behind me with a click and I found myself in an enclosed courtyard which was empty also except that lying on the white paving stones at its centre was the blue scarf I had seen the night before. I walked over to the gate and tried the door but my heart already knew it would be locked. There was no way out either backwards or forwards. I was trapped.

Presently I picked up the scarf and pressed it to my face.

The sun was low in the sky and long shadows danced on the walls. Once again I was tired. I never seemed truly to rest in my sleep and I had begun to notice that each time I awoke I felt increasingly lethargic. I wanted to lie down again and sleep but I knew my body wouldn't allow me that luxury so instead I rose and went to stand in front of the mirror. It had become a ritual, as though I no longer existed without this looking-glass feedback. My body felt completely misshapen. All the clothes I was used to wearing – the little white T-shirts, the short summer skirts that stopped mid-thigh, my Levis – everything seemed to belong to someone else and, as if in confirmation of this fact, as if I needed one, I then felt a definite kick from within. The baby was moving and the kick made me jump as though a volt of electricity had been shot through my body. The look of surprise on my face was palpable. My eyes seemed to grow wide and I smiled at my reflection.

I envied my child its dark watery sack and I thought of the time I had found a cave by the sea when I was seven and of the pool deep within; how dark it had seemed to me then as I stood by its edge and imagined all the strange fish that must swim in its depths. I had been frightened and ran out into the blinding light to find my mother. Now, as I stood in front of the mirror, I thought of my child swimming in a pool such as that; out of sight, protected from the light and the heat, and I wanted to join it, to leave my mother behind and swim in the pool in the depths of the cave.

EMMENTAL

Silky-smooth jacket, pale ochre interior, spherical holes evenly distributed throughout. This cheese has a distinctive if slightly sweet taste and is prone to sweating.

When I thought it was time, I made an appointment for an ultrasound at the hospital. I took one of the city's silver buses as the journey was long and sat opposite an old woman in a black shawl who stared at me over her basket of shopping. Through the smells of petrol and dust I was sure I could detect a strong odour of fish. At first I thought it was coming from her basket, but when we reached my stop and I stood up I could see her basket was empty. She smiled up at me as I stared down at her and her face cracked like dry earth.

The hospital was a tall, white building which stood on one side of a tree-lined square of shops and cafés. The centre of this square was filled with white sand and benches for patients or shoppers to sit on. Groups of young children would stand around this area playing. Some would sit on the ground with old magazines and keyrings with pictures of the Virgin Mary and Jesus enamelled on them and warm cans of fizzy drink spread out in the dust for the visitors to take in with them.

By the time the bus had dropped me off, it was late

afternoon and the building had thrown an awkward shadow out over the square. The city had been transformed into a giant sundial with its buildings marking off the hours. I stood in the four o'clock shade and looked around me. The hospital had peeled in the heat and under the white paint you could see a previous layer of pink as if it were skin. As I stood there, a young girl of no more than thirteen or fourteen came over to me clutching an armful of half-dead flowers. She was very slight with large blue eyes, made all the larger somehow by her thinness.

'Buy some?' she said, thrusting a bunch of spider lilies up at me with a scrawny hand and smiling. She had a baby strapped to her back whose pale head lolled against her as though its spine had been snapped. Saliva dribbled from its mouth. I gave her some money and took the bunch of flowers and she walked away to where her friends stood in a huddle at the side of the square. From behind she looked like one of the bent old women who walk the streets begging for money.

Inside the hospital was momentarily cool and dark after the light of the city. I took instructions from a nurse at the front desk and then followed a series of signs that led me up a stone stairway to the second floor and afterwards along a near-deserted corridor. Coiled hose-pipes hung at regular intervals along the walls and beneath them stood large red buckets of sand with the word 'Fire' written on them. I wondered if the hospital incinerators were in operation and how many soiled sheets and bloodied towels they burnt each day. Doctors were like gods while the fires burnt below. Somewhere far away a fly buzzed frantically against the glass of a window.

Eventually I found the number of the room which was printed on my appointment card and entered through heavy swing doors.

I sat in the waiting-room alone and looked at the posters of pregnant women that were stuck to the walls. All of these women were at various stages of pregnancy, their bodies fermenting and swelling while they waited for the signal that they could move on. My sister had said by the time you had your second or third child you would let anyone put their hands inside you, but these women all looked so serene and intact, as though no one had so much as laid a finger on them.

'You can go in now,' a nurse said, popping her head round one of three doors that led off the waiting-room. 'Through there,' she pointed.

I undressed behind a white screen and then put on a thin green gown which hung over the back of a chair inside the cubicle. When I emerged from behind the curtain the doctor was washing his hands. He told me to get up on the examination table and then he pulled up my gown so that my lower half was naked. He walked to the far side of the room and picked up a tube that lay on the counter, unscrewed its cap and then squirted some clear gel into the palm of his hand.

'I am going to put some of this on your stomach,' he

said, returning to my side and holding his hand out for me to look. 'It will be rather cold.'

He laid the palm of his hand on my skin and smeared the gel with small circular movements. As he rubbed I could feel the size of my stomach under his touch. The reality of it rose like a huge dome in front of me. When I was alone and lying on my bed or standing in front of the mirror, I liked its shape and its size and the way my skin was smooth and taut like a white balloon. The child was forming me, and I the child, and this exchange was a secret between the two of us, but here in this room, with my stomach exposed and the doctor present, I felt it obscene. The child was my secret friend, the kind you read about in books, the kind that lonely children acquire, the kind who do not really exist.

'Do we have to look at it?' I asked.

'It won't harm it.'

'I don't really want us to look. It seems unfair,' I said. 'Like we're spying on it.'

'I have to take a look. If you like you can keep your eyes closed. Now,' he said in his mechanical voice, 'I am going to place this disc on your stomach.'

Despite myself I propped myself up on my elbows so that I could see the monitor more clearly.

'This machine,' the doctor said, patting the metal box, 'fishermen use something very similar to find shoals of fish and then they cast their nets and harvest them just like fruit.' He flicked a switch and immediately I saw a whole series of shadowy silver dots flickering in the arc of my stomach. 'Salmon or sole?' the doctor joked weakly.

'That's it? It doesn't look real.'

'Look carefully. Can you see, this is its head and this is an arm and these are its feet?'

'Yes,' I said, reaching over and touching the warm glass with my fingers.

It was like looking at a picture someone has taken of a ghost which has to be explained.

'It's really there, isn't it?'

'Of course it's there. Look at your stomach.'

I deliberately chose the long route home so I could stop off at the cheese shop. I walked through the streets with their smells of early-evening cooking wafting through the opened shutters. The aroma of boiling meats and cooking fat mingled with that of cigarettes and coffee, and rested on the air along with all the other vapours breathed out by the city over the past few months, gathering layer upon layer. The sky was fading now from pale blue to a darker, more violet shade.

I came to the bridge over the stench-ridden river and began to cross it. The water was again at its lowest ebb and looked thick with an oily effluent mass. It was more like a stagnant pond or a sewer than a river that changed with time, and you could see great clouds of mosquitoes shimmering over it. A crowd had gathered near the middle and people were leaning over the edge, obviously watching something below. I drew nearer and as I did so a young woman walked towards me from the direction of the disturbance. She reminded me of photographs of my mother. She wore a scarf around her head just like my mother used to and had two young children with her who smiled at me as they grew close.

'What's happening?' I asked as she walked past me.

She stopped and turned for a moment. 'Someone's seen a body. The river is being dragged.'

'They're bringing it up?'

The woman nodded. 'Probably a suicide. I saw them fish out a horse once. No legs,' she said as she walked on hurriedly.

I watched as the little group disappeared, the children being pulled along by their mother like two miniature dogs. My curiosity aroused, I went and stood alongside the remaining onlookers.

Below us a police boat floated on the low tide of the river and I watched as two uniformed men released what looked like a long rope down into the water. The rope had a four-pronged hook on the end and I couldn't help thinking of the men who fished from the banks of the river under the chestnut trees. When it rained they would put up coloured umbrellas and some days the line stretched for miles. None of them talked to one another: they just sat and stared at the water. I never saw any of them catch a thing but they would return Sunday after Sunday to cast their lines and sit and wait.

Now I watched as the police pulled the rope up and then threw it out again. They could obviously see something down there in the water that we couldn't, but they couldn't secure it. They threw the rope out a number of times and then suddenly the man who was holding the rope shouted and we could all see that it had grown tight. The man signalled for his partner to start winding the rope in on a pulley that was rigged up on deck. More people had gathered on the bridge now and I could see several had walked down to the riverbank and were sitting on the edge like picnickers.

The light was fading and the water looked black and murky. It seemed to take for ever for the object at the end of the rope to be retrieved, as though the river were bottomless or the body too heavy to pull through the water, and all the time we stood and watched. I could hear murmurs round me, people conjecturing at what the body would look like, whether male or female, young or old. Then suddenly there was a cry and the body emerged, jerked out of the water by one foot, naked, blue and wrapped in weed. It hung in the air, a trophy for the uniformed fishermen, its arms and legs dangling down, and we all stood and stared in silence. All one could tell was that it was a woman.

I walked further up the bridge and leant over as far as I could go. It was almost impossible to see her face but as I stood there one of the policemen pulled the rope and the body swung round almost ninety degrees. I wanted to see her more closely, I wanted to see her face, examine it, but from that distance and in the half-light of evening it was impossible. Now the police placed masks over their noses and mouths. They began to lower the body on to a stretcher on deck. One of them, who wore gloves, grabbed her by the shoulders and then she was laid out and covered with a white sheet. I could see the water seeping through the cotton, outlining her most basic features as if she were a half-finished clay sculpture being kept soft under a wet cloth. The boat started up. They would be taking her to the city morgue to label her and put her away in a cold dark place until the time for burial. I was still holding on to the bunch of flowers I had bought outside the hospital. I threw them now on to the water, then turned my back on the scene and left the small crowd behind me.

Though it was late the shop was still open. As I entered, the bell rang and the cool mossy smell immediately made my body tingle. I hoped to see the owner again. Since my first visit I had returned several times and we had talked on more than one of these occasions. His name was Monsieur Montasio. Each conversation we had, he would teach me something more about cheese.

This evening the shop appeared to be empty; no one was serving and I was the only customer. I walked around, breathing in the cool-sharp air, and then I heard the sound of voices. Several people were talking and laughing. Abruptly the noise stopped and there was silence. I walked over to the door, thinking I should probably leave, when suddenly the old man's head popped up from behind the counter.

'I was downstairs,' he said in apology. 'We're making

some cheese of our own. I'm sorry. We should have locked the door,' and as he spoke he gradually grew taller.

'You make cheese on the premises?'

'In the cellar,' he said, pointing to the floor behind the counter where I imagined a trap door to be. 'Just a few. Most of the space is for storage purposes.'

'Could I buy some?'

'It's not ready yet. Maybe in a few weeks' time. It has to mature.'

The old man allowed me to taste various cheeses and finally I settled on a Swiss Emmental which he recommended.

'You see the holes?' he asked, holding the cheese up for me to see. 'When is a hole not a hole?'

'When it's a half,' I said.

'Ah, you know the joke. Well, to most people a hole is a hole, but of course this is not true. Be a detective and know your quarry! Sniff out your cheese like a true cheesehound. An Emmentalian hole should be round and about the size of an eyeball or a large bullet. Know your holes and you'll find your cheese. Misread the signs and you'll take home an impostor,' he said, putting the Emmental down and washing his hands under a tap. Afterwards he dried his hands, then carefully picked up the Emmental and placed it on a thick wooden board. He took a piece of wire and laid it over the cheese, measuring the cut precisely. 'I'll let you know when our cheese is ready,' he said.

FERMENTATION

When I returned home I went to the kitchen, unwrapped the Emmental and then looked it up in my book. Once again the book gave a fair-enough description of the cheese, but it was particular words that stuck in my mind and made me hungry as I read. Curdling, scalding, pressing, ripening. Words that wrapped round your tongue. And all the time I was reading I was consuming large chunks of Emmental. The salty taste filled my mouth and I rolled the cheese on my tongue and let its flavour spread through me.

This time when I lay down I thought of the body lying in the morgue and its pale milky skin slowly decomposing, and then I thought of the cellars in the cheese shop and of the old man and his staff gathered in the mushroomy silence, mixing the milk, draining and stirring the vast liquid masses, creating their gold. I could almost hear the milk drip, dripping into the metal pails.

I found myself walking through what I perceived to be a fairground. I asked a woman passer-by where I was and she replied that we were in the water-gardens of the Third Empress. I wanted to talk to her further but she said she was searching for her children and then hurried away into the crowd.

I wandered through the throng of people, watching as they flowed to and fro like tides about me. Their reflections shimmered in the many pools lit by roaring torches and a smell of fire filled the air. I caught glimpses of faces I had known and in particular a man's face appeared in my vision. I began to walk cautiously towards him, but as I did so he began to walk in the opposite direction. I followed, trying to keep him within view, but as fast as I walked I could not catch up. At times I lost sight of him altogether and amidst the crowds thought I would never find him again, but, just when I least expected, he would reappear at some distance from me. I would see him playing with a child or talking with a stranger.

I watched as lovers walked hand in hand and gazed upwards at rockets which streaked the sky and filled it with a thousand stars. Old and young, all were nodding and smiling, and the huge milky moon shone down upon them from the distant mountains.

At length I came to a stall which was built like a small theatrical stage. Above was a sign in elaborate gold lettering which read 'Lovely Flutes' and beneath this, sitting on a low chair on top of the slightly raised platform, was a young Japanese girl.

The girl's face was tilted to one side and was clown-white with huge green fish eyes. Her top half was clothed in layers of silk which were pulled up over her knees to expose her legs and the small opening of her sex. I could see her white stockings and then the skin of her thighs and the small triangle of rich dark hair.

She leant back with her hands on the floor behind her and relaxed her legs, and it was as if a flower had unfolded for she had been tattooed in that region with the shape of a full-blown rose. I could see the two perfect pink folds of skin like bruised petals at the centre.

Before her stood a line of men and again I saw the man I had been following. I did not approach him but rather moved to one side to view the scene.

The first man in the queue stood directly before her and then picked up from the table a very fat, long hollow bamboo shoot amongst an array of differently sized ones. He put one end of the tube to his mouth whilst positioning the other as close as possible to the girl's open sex without quite touching it. The man then bent his legs slightly and blew and the girl began to sway her hips from side to side as though following the tickle of the breath being blown down the flute. I could see her thigh muscles move and I wanted to put my hands on them and feel each muscle as it pulled and contracted. I wanted to feel the pulse of her blood and of her body. The man blew harder and the girl's entire body swayed around the stream of air like a snake might sway to the sound of a flute. I could see that the opening of her sex was moist with desire and seemed to grow larger with each breath of air. She looked so warm inside. The man controlled her with the tip of the flute and the warmth of his breath and eventually the girl began to giggle at the tickle of this breath. The man's cock was hard and taut, his erection bulging from beneath his trousers, but once the girl had laughed he immediately passed the flute to the next in line and disappeared inside a small red tent which stood to one side of the stage.

EMMENTAL

In all, I watched eleven men choose a flute and attempt to make the girl laugh in this manner. Three succeeded and each of them passed into the red tent beyond, while the rest disappeared into the crowd. Then I felt someone tapping on my shoulder and when I turned around an old woman stood behind me.

'You want to go inside?'

'Yes,' I said and she took me by the hand and led me to the back of the tent and drew me in.

A long line of girls were kneeling on the floor and a screen with round holes of differing size, each at waist level, stood before them. The girls were licking and sucking at cocks passed through the holes, some of which were fat and stubby and some of which were long and thin.

'The girls all have their preferences,' the woman said. 'I measure them when they enter.' She pulled out a long tape from her pocket. 'And you?' she asked.

I motioned with my hands the size I desired and she led me to a hole about three-quarters of the way up the screen where I knelt down in the dirt to wait. Eventually I watched as the tip of a cock pushed itself through the hole, nervously at first as though it were trying to see what lay beyond. I touched its neat round tip with the end of my tongue and immediately felt it being pushed through harder. I placed my hands against the partition and now leant into the wall, running my tongue up the long shaft of the erection. I knew that the man I had been following was on the other side of the wall and it was him

FERMENTATION

I was sucking on and taking into my mouth and I pushed hard against the wall as I plunged down over his cock, moving my tongue against the taut silky skin until finally the liquid spilled forth and I could hear a groan from the other side of the wall like death.

Outside men were still queuing at the stage and the girl who giggled sat quite still waiting for the next in line to pick up a flute. I stood to one side of the tent at the flap where I had seen the man enter and waited for the man I had been following to emerge. But he did not come. Instead a cripple hobbled out, his back deformed like that of a hunchback and his face twisted into a smile.

ROQUEFORT

A sheep's-milk cheese with a strong piquant flavour sometimes made with rennet from the lining of sheep's stomachs. The greeny-blue veining must have fanned throughout the velvety mass, lending the cheese a dark, throaty quality. You should not buy Roquefort that has a grey complexion or a watery mould.

As my body grew steadily larger, my craving for cheese continued and my desire for stronger and more brackish cheeses increased. I would eat the cheese at lunch and lie down every afternoon to rest. Genuine sleep was illusory. I spoke to my doctor and he gave me iron tablets to take, but it had got to the stage where the only thing my body would allow past my lips was the cheese and even if I did manage to swallow a pill or two they didn't seem to help. Eventually I threw the bottle away.

The old man was very sympathetic and would allow me to rest whenever I visited his shop. He could see how tired I was. One particularly hot day when I arrived he looked at me and shook his head.

'You are too tired to take anything in today. Berthe,' he spoke to the young girl behind the counter, 'go and fetch the chair from upstairs, please.' I heard her climb the stairs to the apartment above and moments later she returned carrying a beautiful wooden chair which he placed at the back of the shop. 'This is your chair,' he said, 'for you only,' and every time I visited the shop thereafter, either he or Berthe or one of the boys would usher me to it. They even placed a cushion on it to make me more comfortable.

The old man taught me much over the months: which cheeses were best during which season, which wine to drink to complement each cheese, how to distinguish a good goat's cheese from a bad, a good Chaumont from one that was inedible.

'With a Roquefort what you are looking for is the distribution of the mould. Examine how much the mould has spread through the cheese's mass. Imagine a peacock fanning its tail and the blue spreading through the sunlight. At the centre is the bird itself. It's the same with this cheese. The fermentation should have begun at the centre and worked its way to the edge,' he said, looking down at my stomach. 'It's really not that different. Your child is growing within you.'

'It had better not be mouldy.'

'Your blood is running through its veins, though. And vice versa. Fermentation is like a swelling. Physical, emotional, edible. It's all the same.'

'And then what happens?'

'The child is born. We eat the cheese. It doesn't really matter. Fermentation is neither the beginning nor the end, but if it goes well then the end is always a much better prospect. A watery Brie or a runny cheese in general is a pleasure to no one. Excessive fermentation. When's your child due?' I laughed at this and the old man smiled. 'You've never spoken about the father.'

'He's not around.'

'Do you want him to be?'

'I don't know. I miss him.'

'He's on your mind?'

'Yes. He's on my mind.'

'You talk to him in your head? You want to be with him? You imagine him coming back?'

'Yes.'

'The sex will be good if he does.' The old man laughed at my expression. 'Sex is always good when you don't know if it's going to be for the last time.'

'This has very little to do with cheese.'

'If there was a cheese shortage and you didn't know whether the cheese you were eating would be the last taste you'd ever get?'

'I do miss him,' I said. 'But I can't decide whether I miss him because he isn't here.'

'That's how it's supposed to be.'

'Yes, and when they come back you're supposed to be happy because you no longer have to miss them. The hunger vanishes.'

'And the pleasure gone?'

I nodded my head.

'As I was saying, excessive fermentation is not good. Now if you'll excuse me,' he said, 'I have to do some work downstairs.'

When the old man had gone I asked the albino boy, 'How many cheeses are there?'

FERMENTATION

'Over one thousand,' he said, 'and new ones are being created every week. The smaller the world becomes, the more cheese there seems to be. You'll never taste them all, but try the Roquefort. It's the king of cheeses.'

'The king?'

'It has the blue blood of royalty running through its veins,' he said, pointing to a tall cylindrical tower in the centre of the counter. When the boy cut into the cheese I could feel the knife slicing through the thin rind and then slipping into the supple body of the piece as easily as if it were splicing me open. He cut a perfectly sized wedge and gently levered it out so that it balanced on the flat edge of his knife. Now I could peek inside the cheese and see, set against the darkness of the rind, how the greater mass was uniformly shot throughout with a light greeny-blue veining. It was exactly as the old man had described the perfect Roquefort.

'Roquefort is a true cheese-lover's cheese. Its veins will run through you,' the boy said, giving me a small piece to taste. 'Test it against the tip of your tongue. Right there,' he said, sticking his own tongue out and tapping the end of it. 'It's very good, isn't it? A sort of complex flavour. Monsieur says this is the best month for Roquefort.'

'Has he always owned this shop?'

'No. Berthe's father used to own it. The shop could have been hers but she sold it to Monsieur. He was a friend of the family and used to be a carpenter by trade. He built sets for the theatre.' The albino boy blinked and then handed me the package of cheese.

ROQUEFORT

This time I couldn't wait to get the cheese home and had to stop off in the park to taste it. I found a seat near to where some children were playing and sat down. The cheese had already begun to melt and I scooped up a large piece with my fingers and stuck them in my mouth. I could feel the soft mouldy tubes against my tongue, their penetratingly sharp taste, and it wasn't long before I had finished the whole piece off, even down to licking the wrapping where the cheese had oozed out against the paper.

The house stood in isolation in the middle of wide lawns that stretched to the hills. Someone had built a huge bonfire which towered menacingly on the lawn at the back of the house. I could see it from where I was hiding. Whoever had built it had spent days on it. You could see where tree trunks had been dragged across the lawns and, as a final touch, a small stepladder had been propped up against it which led to the top.

I stood on tiptoe and that way I could see straight into the house through the leaves of the bushes behind which I was hidden. A woman was sitting in a chair before a large mirror. She was a young woman, in her mid-twenties. Her skin was smooth and she wore her blonde hair in a bob that only just touched the nape of her neck. Next to the woman was a small table. That was all.

A black Ford car slowed down the gravel driveway and then came to a standstill. The engine cut and a man got out. I ducked down into the undergrowth until he had reached the back door and let himself in. After several minutes I rose up to peer through the window, half expecting the woman to have disappeared, but she was still there, sitting impassively in the chair.

The man entered the room. I could see he held a small bowl in one hand and had a blue towel and something darker draped over one arm. The woman did not turn round but remained staring at her reflection in the mirror. I could not tell but I did not think she even registered his entry.

The man now stood beside her. He took out a small object from the breast pocket of his shirt. It was a razor and he proceeded to draw it up and down a leather strap. That was the object he had been carrying along with the towel. He was sharpening the razor's edge. When he had finished I saw him put the razor down and pick up the small bowl. I saw his lips move as if in speech and the woman immediately tilted her head back. She could still see herself in the mirror. The man lifted his arm and she closed her eyes. I saw his lips move again and at once she re-opened them. Then he took a small squat brush from the bowl and began to lather her face. He drew the brush over her pale cheeks and dabbed at her upper lip. He stroked under her chin. Finally, when her face was covered in the thick creamy lather, he placed the bowl and brush to one side and picked up the sharpened razor.

He held the razor up between his fingertips, so that the woman could see the gleaming silver blade in the mirror, and then he placed its edge against the skin of her cheek and drew it down in one long, even stroke. He did this several times and each time I could feel the skin tingling down my spine.

When it came to her neck he held her head with one hand as he poised the razor's edge at her throat with the other. Momentarily he caught her eyes in the reflection, then swiftly he moved round to the back of the chair, tilted her head right back and drew the knife up the tight skin of her neck. The woman's mouth opened as the razor pulled over her skin and her hands clasped the arms of the chair tightly.

I could see the man was aroused. He pushed the girl out of the chair and slid it to one side. Holding the girl by her hair, he leant her body against the ledge under the mirror. With one hand he kept her pinned down, with the other he tore down her pants and unzipped his flies. His cock was fully erect and I watched as he pushed it inside her cunt, all the time keeping her face to the mirror and watching her as he shoved into her harder and harder and her soft pink tongue flicked and licked the glass. Then I saw him pick up the razor again and I watched as he raised the blade and then swiftly drew it across her throat. She slumped forward immediately like a veal calf, her legs buckling beneath her, blood spurting out and hitting the mirror, whilst at the same time the man's whole body jerked into her, making her move like a puppet. When he finally withdrew, he slipped the knife into his pocket and then, wrapping his arms around the girl's waist, lifted her up on to his shoulders. I could see the blood was still pumping out, soaking into the man's white T-shirt. He brought her out into the garden where he laid her on top of the bonfire and then crouched down to light a match. Once the fire was alight the man walked away.

At first the flames were small, like bright parrot tulips, but gradually they rose higher and began to lick at the girl's arms and legs and I could see how her face was melting in the shimmering heat, being devoured down to the bone.

'Do you like fire?' a voice came from behind me. I turned round to see the man standing by the bushes. 'You can't see properly from there. Why don't you move closer?' he said, taking me by the arm. He walked me across the lawn and then stopped at some distance from the fire. 'Do you think this is close enough?' he asked.

'Yes, I think so.'

'No. You are wrong,' he said, walking me closer again and then stopping.

'How about this?'

'This is a good view,' I said.

'But still a little too far, wouldn't you say? Better closer still,' and he led me so close that now I could feel the heat of the flames against my face and the smell of the burning body stung in my nostrils.

'This is a good spot,' he said.

'Yes. Yes, this is very good too.'

'You can smell the flesh burning, can't you?'

'Yes, I can smell it.'

'Fire is cleansing. It cleanses the air. It kills off impurities. Bodies should never be buried. They breed in the earth. Fire is the final solution.'

We moved again and this time when we stopped we were only centimetres from the flames which leaped up from the inferno. The woman who lay at the heart of the fire was nothing but a blackened skeleton and I could hear her bones cracking. Soon she would disappear altogether, her body turned to ash.

'Ash is softer than skin,' he said. 'Is your skin soft?'

'Yes,' I said.

'Soft enough?'

'Yes,' I said.

The man was pressing up against me and then his hands ripped at the back of my dress. He put his arms around my waist to act as a support while he pushed himself inside me. I tried to struggle free, to prise his hands open, and then suddenly I was aware that the moment I succeeded, the moment I found a way to make him release his grasp, I would fall straight into the fire. The choice was mine.

I awoke to an unnerving silence. The children were no longer playing. No one was there. I looked at my watch which read 6pm. I had been sleeping on the bench for over three hours and no one had thought to wake me to ask if I was ill or needed help. They probably thought I was a tramp and that the bench was my home. I was very tired, my dress was wet from sweat and where my skin had been exposed to the sun it was red and sore. It took me a considerable amount of time to walk back to my apartment. I shuffled along the streets exhausted and sweating. I wanted nothing but to reach my bed and lie down and close my eyes and sleep a deep sleep. And yet I knew that when I returned home my body would begin its craving again. It was a hopeless cycle.

It was at this stage that the child's movements appeared to lessen. After the first time I had felt it kick, it would repeat its aggressive action with apparent vengeance almost every day, but now this activity waned. I believed the child had become calmer or perhaps it too had begun to feel the heat and had grown lethargic like its mother.

GAMMELOST

A Norwegian cheese reeking of juniper berries. The mould is introduced to the cheese by piercing it with long metal needles. It has an overpowering flavour with a pungent aroma and unless eaten in small quantities bears a punishing aftertaste.

I walked through the city but I do not remember where I went or what I saw. The city had receded and my dreams were what I remembered. My world was being turned inside out: the waking hours vanishing or coming back to me in glimpses, the dreaming hours recalled in minute detail and mad, vivid colours. Or maybe both worlds merged but I could no longer tell where reality ended and the dreams began. The summer dragged on; July, August, September. I was floating at sea and the line on the horizon where the sea ended and the sky began melded into one. Perhaps it had always been like that but I had never noticed.

It was the hottest day yet. The thermometer measured 42 degrees at midday, the air was thick with flies and the stench on the streets had reached unbearable proportions. The army had been ordered to clear away the rubbish. They patrolled the streets at night, standing by their trucks with guns slung round their waists like exotic pieces of jewellery. It was all cosmetic. The smell clung to the air and had seeped into the buildings and the pavements and the skin of the people. Our skin was porous and, just like the cheese which wept out its salt, so our skin drank in the rank, fetid atmosphere. It was all related. The smell of the city was in our sweat and the news broadcasts told of water shortages and bulletins advised us to share baths and not to water the plants.

The only thing that retained water was the body I lived in. I was hiding a secret reservoir that no one could tap, but the penance for this clandestine activity was that I could hardly move because I was so heavy, and my ankles had swollen so that it was painful to walk. I felt like a slug and yearned like Christian for a release from my burden.

That particular morning I discovered an old measuring tape in one of my cupboards. I slipped it round my waist but I could not make the ends meet. I was a custard marrow, a shiny dark aubergine: plants that slowly fill with liquid until their thick skins are set to split.

After my shower I left the apartment and went for a walk. I found a café and sat outside in the shade of a large green umbrella. I closed my eyes. When I opened them again Justine was sitting at one of the far tables. She was with a group of friends, talking and laughing. I sat and watched her ordering coffee and cakes and then a man came up to her and bent down and kissed her on the right side of her face. Eventually he turned round to where I was sitting and stared right at me. It was Serge.

I stood up and from my table hailed a taxi, but instead

of telling the driver to take me back to the apartment I told him to go to rue Trebec. I wanted to see the old man. As the car pulled off I turned round in my seat. I could see Serge standing on the pavement. His hands were in his pockets and he was staring at the car as it drew away. I thought I saw him shrug and then I thought I saw him smile.

Berthe was standing behind the counter when I walked in. She had taken to touching my stomach whenever I visited the shop and resting her ear against me, believing she might hear its heart beat like an African drum. 'It's still sleeping,' she'd say. 'Maybe I'll hear it next time, eh?'

But this time when I entered she looked at me and immediately directed me to the chair.

'What's wrong?'

'Is he here?'

'I'll call him,' she said. 'Just keep an eye on the shop.'

She disappeared into the back and moments later the old man came downstairs.

'Come up. I'll help you.'

He took me by the arm and together we walked through to the back of the building and up a narrow staircase. He showed me into a small room without much furniture. There was a bed and a table with books on it. I sat down on the bed.

'So?'

'I saw him. I didn't know he was back.'

'You've been crying.'

FERMENTATION

'I feel ugly. Look at me.'

'You're pregnant. You're fat. But you're not ugly.'

'I'm a ripe cheese?'

'Sounds good to me.'

The old man poured out two glasses of wine and handed me one. His hands were ancient. I noticed their veins and the brown mottled marks on their skin. 'The wine will do you good,' he said. 'Drink it.'

'Why do you live like this?' I said, looking round the room.

'I don't want anything else. I don't need it.'

'You must want something.'

'I'm happy here. I like the work . . .'

'What about a lover?'

'You're taken,' he said, laughing.

'Would you have had me?'

'You wouldn't have had me. More to the point, isn't it? Stick to what you really love.'

'But aren't you ever lonely?'

The old man looked down and for some reason I looked down with him, but there was nothing on the floor.

'Berthe?' I said.

He looked up again. 'Yes. Berthe.'

'But you never said.'

'I thought you knew.' He put his glass down on the table. 'I've known her since she was a child. Are you shocked?'

'I just didn't see it,' I said.

'I keep telling her to find someone her own age but she laughs.' The old man looked over at me. 'Lie down for a while. I think you should rest.'

I lay down and he came over and brushed his hand over my head.

'You'll be fine,' he said. 'Believe me. I know.'

I closed my eyes. I heard him leave the room and go downstairs. I heard noises from the shop below and outside on the street and then I fell asleep. It was the first deep sleep I had experienced for what seemed like weeks. I slept all through the afternoon and I did not dream.

Later, when I went downstairs, the old man was waiting for me.

'Here,' he said. 'Gammelost. You'll like it. It's good and strong. The neat whisky of cheeses.'

'Thank you.'

'Try and rest more,' he said. 'You want this baby to be properly fermented, don't you?'

I nodded.

'So take care of yourself.'

After I had stepped out on to the street he locked the shop door behind me and waved at me through the window as he hung a sign on the door. The sign read, 'Closed.'

It was dark and the street-lamps had been turned on and drew out deep pools of light. I don't know what it was that made me take a different route home, but instead of heading towards the river I turned down one of the many narrow streets and walked for several minutes before branching off again on to a second road, one I thought would bring me out close to the river. This second street must have led me in the opposite direction, however, for very soon I was lost, walking through a district I had never visited before.

I was alerted to a new smell, one of spices and herbs and sweet incense lingering and mingling in the heat. A short way ahead of me a door opened and a figure stepped out. The figure was swathed from head to toe in black. I could only see this person from behind and could not tell if it was male or female, but some instinct prompted me to follow him or her and so we began to wind our way through the labyrinthine maze where at length this figure was joined by a second. The two walked ahead of me for some time and I followed them past glittering window displays of televisions and hi-fi equipment and shops selling trays of strange-coloured sweets. The figures were my guides until quite suddenly they stopped and looked round. It was only then that I saw their faces, saw that they were wearing beak-like metal masks which glinted in the evening sun and made them invisible. They stared at me for what seemed like minutes as though they were passing judgment, although neither spoke or conferred in any way, and then, their decision made, they turned once more to the street ahead and continued walking. Now, more of these women emerged from doorways and side streets and I realised we were all heading towards a square where a market had been set up with coloured lights strung between the stalls. The square was full of the beaked women wandering through the stalls of many-coloured fish and seafruits piled high. There were tables of sunset-pink shrimps and crates of langoustine and shimmering skate and everything smelt of dark seaweed and salt. The women passed through the stalls, their dark eyes peering from the slits in their masks like those of a shark.

I stood transfixed for a while on the outskirts of this scene, and the people came and went, dancing in dark patterns around me, and through the murmur and the noise of the market I heard a sound like that of a child crying, only I couldn't see any child, only the blackness of the invisible women moving around me, brushing against me. I turned and walked quickly away, all the time feeling that they were following me. I tried to recall the way I had come and walked as fast as I could, retracing my steps, looking for a familiar street sign, but everything was foreign to me; everywhere I looked I could only see strange writing and the curls and waves of the letters made no sense. I stopped for a moment to catch my breath and a man came up to me and asked if I was lost.

'Yes,' I replied and he asked me where I needed to go and I gave the name of the street where the cheese shop was situated.

'It's very near,' he said. 'Come with me and I'll show you.'

FERMENTATION

I followed him until we reached the cheese shop where he bade me goodnight.

When I returned to the apartment it was dark and I didn't see Serge standing in a small recess in the shadows of the stairwell. I had passed him before he spoke my name.

'Hello Odissa,' he said.

His voice was quiet and it startled me. He walked up to where I stood and put his hand out as though he were going to touch my arm, and my whole being filled with butterflies. We stood and stared at each other in the dim light.

'How long have you been back?'

'Since this morning. I was saying goodbye to the others. I was on my way to see you.'

'Well, I'm still here, as you can see.'

'Why did you run away like that?'

'I didn't like what I saw.'

Serge didn't answer. Instead he cast his eyes over my body and then he stepped closer and brushed his lips against mine. I felt his hands slip down over my stomach and my body spin round like a schoolroom globe. His hands spread out over me and he kissed my eyes closed. He was lifting my dress up and stroking my thighs.

'Tell me you didn't sleep with her,' I whispered. 'Tell me.'

'Her body was soft,' he said. 'I kissed her mouth and her breasts,' he said, kissing my mouth and then opening my dress and putting his mouth to my breasts. I could feel he was hard and he pressed himself against me. The child was between us and he began turning me round just like the first time. 'I kissed her face. I ran my tongue against her skin, over her scars,' he said, and I could feel how his hands had touched her and made love to her. He was pushing himself into me now and I saw her face in front of me and felt his hands touching my face and my whole body melting.

Afterwards I walked past him and opened the door to my apartment. Serge stood on the landing. 'You wanted the truth. You liked watching. You were there all the time.'

'Yes,' I said.

'I want to come back, Odissa.'

'Do you?'

'Please?' He spoke the words softly.

'I'm very tired,' I said, before closing the door and locking it behind me.

I did not switch the lights on. I put my bags down on the floor and went into the bathroom. My face was burning and I splashed cold water over and over against my skin. When I had finished I came out and stood by the window in the dark. I stood slightly back so that no one could see me, and yet I could see out. Serge was across the street, leaning against a wall. He lit a cigarette. The glow from the flame illuminated his face. He did not look up at the window but stood and smoked his cigarette. At one point he walked a little way down the street, and for a moment I thought he was leaving, but then he stopped and turned around and came and leant against the wall once again. I watched him as he stood there drawing on his cigarette, running his hand through his hair, and then he threw his cigarette on the ground and very slowly got down on his knees. It was only then that he looked up at my window.

I took one step forward. Serge did not move from where he knelt. He held his face up towards my window and the light from the street-lamp shone down touching his face and hair. I knew he could see me and I stood there and stared down at him. I remained like that for some time and then I turned away and went through to the kitchen.

I sat down at the table and took the cheese out from my basket and began to cram the food into my mouth, pushing it in with my hands, hardly stopping to chew before I swallowed and crammed more and more in. The cheese was strong and I could feel my mouth smarting against the assault of the rich salty paste. When I had finished I wrapped the remaining crumbs back in the paper and went to put them away for later.

My waters burst midway between the table and the fridge. I could feel warmth rinsing down between my legs and when I looked down a huge pool had formed on the dark blue tiles.

I remember opening the door and then calling the ambulance and afterwards going to the window and looking out but the street was empty. I lay down on the floor of my bedroom amongst the cushions and closed my eyes. I had to count but the numbers didn't make sense and I kept losing my place as the contractions rode over me. Eventually two men arrived. They told me their names and asked if I could walk downstairs and when I said I couldn't they brought a stretcher up and made me lie down while they carried me outside to the ambulance like some giant stranded sea creature.

I remember some of the journey to the hospital, how fast we sped through the streets, but most of all I remember the sound of the rain. I remember listening to the wheels tearing through the wet streets and the sound of the water beating down on the ambulance roof. The two men smiled uncontrollably and as they man-oeuvred me from the ambulance into the hospital they stopped for an instant so that I could feel a few drops of the water on my face. The air smelt fresh and cool.

Immediately nurses in tall white hats like crowns made from snow took my clothes and shaved me and then they pushed me down one corridor after another. I could hear their squeaky shoes padding against the cold white linoleum and the sound of the wheels.

The birthing room was shiny like the inside of a cool crystal star. They laid me down on a high bed in the centre of the room and stretched me out. First they hitched up one leg into a stirrup and then the other.

'You must keep breathing,' a voice said. 'Take deep breaths. Deep. Deep.'

The pain washed over me, dragging me down like the

tide of the sea. I felt the waves moving over me and I tried to swim above them, tried to breathe in time to the waves, but each new intake of air felt as though I were drawing breath for the first and last time. When the pain receded I took in more of my surroundings. When the pain began again my whole being was centred round my sex as it stretched and opened wider and wider, sucking me in. I tried to remember Serge's face, to bring him in front of me and focus on his eyes. If I held his gaze I could keep my face above water, but the moment I let it go I felt myself sinking, the water folding in soft pleats above my head. I could feel the blood pumping and hear the rain outside. My whole being was separating, splitting open like a ripe chestnut, and the water was trickling and seeping and endlessly falling. Miles and miles of fresh grey water above and beneath me. My clothes and hair were wet. The rain was streaming down. I could feel it seeping into the ground and collecting in underground caverns, flowing in rivers and streams and forming dark lakes in caves beneath me. Bridges no longer spanned rivers, signposts no longer pointed to roads, rivers no longer flowed like ribbons. The water had risen and overcome them all. You couldn't tell where the seas ended and the sky began. You couldn't tell. Things were too dark. And the fish swam through it all: steely blue swordfish, billowing skate, sleek grey dolphins and strange white fish that swam at the bottom of the darkest oceans, all soft bodied, all blindly feeling their way in the dark; electric eels with scabrous teeth.

GAMMELOST

Fat black eels that slithered and curled through the shallows sensing the presence of blood, the liquid smell of suppuration, and when at last they found me they gnawed and consumed my soft stomachy flesh leaving only a translucent sack of tender skin. They were eating me out bit by bit.

Nurses bent over, their faces smiling close to mine. 'You're doing well,' their voices said. 'Take deep breaths. The head is showing now.' And then they turned to each other and shook their heads. 'Her husband should be here,' they said, as though I were deaf. 'I ate my placenta. It's full of nourishment, you know. I took it home and fried it with eggs.' I could see their mouths opening and closing and could hear the words as they walked around me. One of them was brandishing a long silvery needle.

'Push down hard. Push!' she said, her white crown bobbing up and down like foam on the water. I could feel myself pushing out into the sea and then I caught in a rip and the tide swept me further into the water. I knew I was drifting and a terror seized me that I would not be able to swim back to shore. I was losing my strength and each vein in my body was straining against the weight that was dragging me down and I kept pushing against the body of water, against the stone which was dragging me down. I wanted to rest, to lie at the bottom of the ocean, on this dark sticky bed, with the boom of the waves over me and the seaweed wrapping around me. Keep breathing. 'Push,' they repeated as though I were deaf and I pushed at their hands as they walked around me, against the weight of the water, through the black corridor and the huge dark orifice. Keep breathing, keep breathing. I pushed them away and I pushed upwards and then suddenly I heard the sound of panting in my ear. It was the sound of my own breath and from the shore where I lay I looked back and saw a huge fish jump from the sea and fly through the air, sunlight catching its long feathery fins.

The child was born shortly after midnight. The doctor held her up by her feet and she hung in the air like an object retrieved from the sea. They laid her on my stomach and I touched her tiny hands and feet. 'You can rest now,' they said. I remember they pushed me out of the room and bathed me and laid me down in a bed. The child rested in a cot beside me, her small hands spreading out towards the light.

HANDMADE CHEESE

A pale, delicate cream cheese. Often best prepared by grinding salt and pepper over it and eating with fresh bread.

I craved cheese only once after the birth. It was shortly after I returned to the apartment with the child. She had suckled from my breasts and where my milk had spilled I caught a few drops with my fingers and licked off the sweet liquid. My breasts were large and engorged with milk. Sometimes at night when she had drunk her fill, in order that I could relieve the weight I would run a bath and crouch down on all fours in the warm water like a cow in a pond while the milk seeped out turning the bath water white. And then I read in my manual that I could actually collect my milk. The process was similar to massaging the teat of a cow. I had to cup each breast in turn and tease the milk out in drops until it flowed evenly. I placed the milk in a bowl and when that was done the idea came to me to make a small homemade cheese out of it. The old man had given me some rennet and I stirred this into my milk and then let the mixture set. Afterwards I tied the mixture up in a small muslin bag over the sink and let it drip.

The cheese tasted mild and slightly watery. I spread it

on some bread and sprinkled salt over it to bring out the flavour and when I had finished I lay down on the bed with the child beside me in her cot. I wasn't tired and for a time I lay and stared at her sleeping. Her face was so perfect. Her skin was clear and I liked to listen to the sound of her breathing.

I walked though lemon fields in the hills above Tuscany. They were streaked red with poppies and the heat of late autumn scumbled the colours, bleeding the red.

The chapel stood shaded from the glare of the sun between two cedar trees. I walked around the outside brushing my hand against the cool stone until I came to a window of clear glass through which I could see the altar. It was set very simply with a wooden cross on a white cloth and a small vase of lilies. The light from a stained window above the altar fell down and formed a pool of red on the cold stone floor. I saw all this and then as my eyes grew accustomed to the light I noticed a painting on one of the white stucco walls.

The Annunciation. Mary, dressed in a pale blue mantle; sitting in a small portico of slender Corinthian columns. In front of her, bowing slightly, stood an angel with feathered wings, robed in translucent vermilion. Mary looked to the ground while the angel peered upwards at her face in a gaze of the most curious nature. It transfixed me and it was only after staring at this painting for several minutes that I noticed in the dim background there was a door, which led to a room, a room with a bed inside.

The angel whose hand was outstretched motioned for Mary to stand up, then took her by the hand and led her through into the bedroom. They began to undress. The angel's robes slipped off easily and fell in a pile along with Mary's thin blue dress. The angel then lay down on the bed and stretched out his legs amongst a huge scattering of pillows which cushioned his wings. Mary climbed on top of him, her legs on either side of his waist. Her back was straight and I could see the tiny bones that made up her vertebrae through her pale skin. She took a clasp out of her hair and it fell blackly down the cream of her skin like a rope of thick treacle.

Mary bends down now, kissing the angel's stomach, running her tongue up the centre of his body, and all the while her body is moving up and down as her whole being rotates round her mouth. The angel places his hands on her head and runs and digs his fingers through her thick black hair.

Slowly then she moves up his body until her legs are either side of his face and she is hovering above it. I can see how he tries to raise his mouth to touch her there, but her hands keep him firmly pinned down. She is enjoying seeing him strain to eat her.

She moves down towards him and his head arches up. She pulls away and then she lowers herself down again. Little by little she lowers herself closer until finally his tongue slips up between her legs, up into her. The muscles of her slender, crouching legs stiffen visibly. Her whole body tightens as his tongue feels its way into the wet of her flesh and I can see how his sex has grown and hardens.

He begins to push her down his body. His hands are clasped around her waist guiding her down until finally he enters her. The blue counterpane is twisted between them.

Afterwards they rise and dress, then step out into the covered portico. Mary takes her seat, the angel positions himself in front of her, bends his knee and kneels and then very gently, very slowly, unfolds his beautiful golden wings.

I awoke to the sound of the child. Her cry was soft and I picked her up from the cot and held her close to me.

In the days that followed I tried to find Serge. I went to his apartment but when I reached it I found the door boarded up and a sign from the council saying no one was to enter. I walked through the city with the child wrapped up under my coat, asking in all the familiar places whether anyone had seen him or knew of his whereabouts, but most of the performers had left for the winter. Some told me Serge had gone also, some said he was still here. Finally I visited the fountain with the three stone fishes. I sat on the edge of the pool and looked into the water. A few golden leaves had drifted down from the surrounding trees and now lay at the bottom, turning black at the edges.

HANDMADE CHEESE

I packed up the apartment and my suitcases and bought a travelling box for the chameleon. I also visited the cheese shop. Berthe and the old man took turns holding the child and both agreed she was a beautifully fermented specimen; a little early, but most important of all not too ripe. 'Send me your address,' the old man said, 'when you know where you're staying.'

The train journey was longer than I remembered. It is one of those laws. The journey back is always longer than the journey forward. The child slept most of the way and when she did cry I would walk her up and down the corridor and people smiled and touched her face.

When we arrived at Lourdes we took the bus up into the mountains to Cauterets. I could see snow on the peaks. At first we stayed in the hotel but afterwards I found a small apartment in the main square.

You want to know, did he come back? The question is still to be answered. At night when the child is asleep I stand by the window and wait. I think I will see him again. Last night I lit a candle and placed it in the window. I sat with the child in my arms and watched as a moth flew down from a dark corner of the room. It was attracted by the flame and danced around the fire on the tips of its wings. It could not escape unless I extinguished the flame.

In the morning I fed its body to the lizard.